Undressed

A COUNTRY ROADS NOVELLA

WITHDRAWN

SHANNON RICHARD

FOREVER
YOURS

New York Boston

Copyright © 2015 by Shannon Richard
Excerpt from *Undone* copyright © 2013 by Shannon Richard
Excerpt from *Undeniable* copyright © 2013 by Shannon Richard
Cover design by Elizabeth Turner
Cover photograph from Shutterstock
Cover copyright © 2015 by Hachette Book Group

Forever Yours
Hachette Book Group
1290 Avenue of the Americas
New York, NY 10104
Hachettebookgroup.com
Twitter.com/foreverromance

First ebook and print on demand edition: February 2015

Forever Yours is an imprint of Grand Central Publishing.
The Forever Yours name and logo are trademarks of Hachette Book Group, Inc.

The publisher is not responsible for websites (or their content) that are not owned by the publisher.

The Hachette Speakers Bureau provides a wide range of authors for speaking events. To find out more, go to www.hachettespeakersbureau.com or call (866) 376-6591.

ISBN 978-1-4555-6100-1 (ebook edition)
ISBN 978-1-4555-9044-5 (print on demand edition)

To my brother, Ronald Richard,
You've watched out for me from the very start
and you've never stopped.
I hope you know how much that means to me.

Acknowledgments

It's hard to believe that the Country Roads journey started only three years ago. I've had an overwhelming amount of support from my family and friends, all of whom continue to go above and beyond to help in all my writing endeavors. I will never be able to thank any of you enough, not even if I told you every minute of every day.

Undressed couldn't have been written without the feedback from one of my closest friends, Katie Crandall. Thank you for reading along the way and being an amazing sounding board. Thank you for helping me brainstorm into the wee hours of the morning. Thank you for loving my characters as much as I do.

It's always amazing when we come across people in our lives who we click with immediately. Jessica Lemmon, I feel as if we've been friends for years and years. Thank you for always being just a text away, and for all the FaceTime babble sessions with wine. You are simply marvelous darling.

So many evenings over the last couple months consisted of conversations of me running ideas past my mother. Antoinette

Richard, thank you for always being there to listen to me and offer more than a few words of wisdom.

There were many phone calls to my father Ron Richard, my brother, Ronald Richard, and more than a few discussions with Tony Silcox about all things sports-related. Thank you all for taking the time to talk things out with me.

Another person who never hesitates to give me feedback is the ever-amazing Nikki Rushbrook. Thank you for being a beta reader. Your thoughts and opinions are valued in more ways than you know.

None of this would be possible without my agent, Sarah E. Younger. You took a chance on me and I hope you know that I will always remember it, I will always appreciate it, and I will always be thankful for you and your guidance. Your constant encouragement and enthusiasm for my writing means the absolute world to me.

The art department at Grand Central Publishing continually blows me away—my covers are gorgeous and I love them beyond words. And to the rest of the team that puts so much time and effort into my books, especially my publicist, Julie Paulauski.

And last, but certainly not least, I have to thank my editor, Megha Parekh. You've championed me from the very beginning. You saw something in my writing that you believed in. You heard my voice and you made it stronger. Working with you is always a pleasure, and I will forever be grateful for everything that you've done for me.

Undressed

Chapter 1

Strip, Shoot, or Truth . . .

Truth: when was the last time you had sex?"

Abby Fields stared across the table at Logan James, trying to figure out how anything that was happening was even possible. This was the most bizarre Valentine's Day of her life. She was stranded in a log cabin in the middle of Tennessee, with a gorgeous man, playing a drinking game.

This couldn't be right. He didn't even like her.

To say that they didn't exactly get along would be an understatement. She was pretty sure it had been his mission to make her job as complicated as possible.

It had been three months since Abby had accepted the position with the Jacksonville Stampede's public relations department. Three months since she'd left her job in Washington, D.C., and headed south to Florida for a better paycheck—and there was the added perk of being closer to her best friend. But if she'd thought for one second that she was leaving the ego stroking and stress behind her, she'd been wrong.

Hockey players were no better than politicians.

Though to be fair, not all of the guys were bad. It was about a fifty-fifty split. Some were cooperative and helpful, willing to listen, offer a friendly smile, could carry on a conversation without scowling at her.

Logan was not one of those guys.

Yet here she was, sitting across from him and debating her next move.

Strip? Well, she was already down to her skirt and camisole. The next thing she took off was going to reveal red lace. That was all she needed, for Logan James to see her panties…because chances were, they would be hitting the floor, too.

Shoot? More alcohol wasn't looking like a good choice. She'd already had four shots of the whiskey, but her inhibitions hadn't been lowered that much to have influenced the disappearance of her clothes. That had been a decision she'd made all on her own.

Truth? He already thought she was uptight and repressed; all she needed was to confirm it with the fact that she hadn't had sex in over a year…and even that hadn't been very satisfying.

"Pick one, Red, that's how the game goes."

Logan was the only one on the team who didn't call her Ms. Fields or Abby. It didn't bother her at all. She was sure there had been way worse nicknames for her, and one based on her auburn hair color was not a bad one. Besides, she really hated being called Ms. Fields because it reminded her of Mrs. Fields, the cookies.

Sweet and warm…things that in no way described her.

Though the way Logan was looking at her might challenge that last statement. She was feeling more than a little *warm* as she looked into those green-gold eyes of his that sparkled from across the table. Then there were his lips that quirked up to the side. He had a sinful mouth, one that promised to do wicked things.

She was used to him scowling at her, none too pleased to be in the same room as her let alone talking to her, but he wasn't frowning now.

Nope.

The guy had a killer smile when he chose to use it, and when it was paired with that jaw of his that was dusted with five-o'clock shadow?

Yeah, good God the man was attractive.

She wanted him. Wanted him more than she'd wanted a man in a very long time. *Too* long of a time. And when had she ever not gone for something she wanted?

Well, she wasn't going to start that nonsense now.

The next two things Abby did shocked the hell out of both of them, as evident by the fact that his eyebrows climbed up his forehead.

One: she reached across the table and grabbed the shot, taking it in one fell swoop.

Second: she scooted the chair back and stood. She unzipped her skirt and pushed it down her thighs, adding it to the pile that included her hair clip, blazer, shoes, and blouse. There were now just as many of her things littering the floor as Logan's—he'd lost his jacket, tie, socks, shoes, and belt.

She reached for the bottom of her camisole next, lifting it over her head and tossing it at him. He caught it before it hit him in the face, pulling it away as his eyes did a slow skim of her body. That mouth of his turned predatory as he took in her red bustier and lace panties, and black thigh-high stockings.

"Damn, Red." The whisper that left his mouth was one of awe.

Abby slipped on her red high heels again before she walked to the other side of the table. She only clocked in at five-foot-two and she was going to use those extra five inches that her shoes provided to her advantage.

Plus, they were really freaking sexy.

Logan pushed his chair back, giving her just enough space to stand in front of him.

"You wrapped up in red lace...Happy Valentine's Day to me." He reached out and his hands skimmed her thighs, working up to her hips where he fingered the straps before he started to unsnap them. He had big hands, strong and powerful, callused and rough, and...oh God, so perfect. She wanted them all over her body.

This was when Abby did the *third* most shocking thing of the night: she climbed up onto his lap and straddled him.

Yeah, Logan wanted her all right. His cock was hard and pressing up into her core. She shifted closer and he groaned. His hands tightened on her hips, holding her in place, and he looked into her eyes. His gaze was hot and intense, not wavering in the slightest. She moved her hands to his hair, her fingers sliding between the dark brown strands.

"It's been a while," she finally answered as she leaned in close. "Truth: do you want to change that?"

"Abso-fucking-lutely." And with that he claimed her mouth. She moaned as his tongue found hers. He tasted like whiskey, warm and earthy. His hands slid to her back and he started working the many hooks at the back of her bustier. A moment later it fell away from her body and he threw it to the side.

He stood, his chair sliding back along the wooden floors, and sat her down on top of the table. She placed her hands behind her on the table for balance as his hands skimmed up her body. He palmed her breasts, his thumbs rasping over her nipples.

She closed her eyes, her head falling back on her shoulders.

"Truth: do you have any idea how long I've wanted you?" The question came out hoarse, like he was barely in control of anything let alone his voice.

Abby's head came up and she looked at him. "Before tonight I thought you couldn't stand me."

He shook his head as he moved his hands to her belly. "Appearances can be deceiving. For example, who would've thought that you'd have something like this underneath those business skirts?" he asked as he continued his downward journey to her thighs and traced the lace tops of her stockings.

"I like expensive lingerie."

"That's interesting, because I like *you* in expensive lingerie." He leaned forward, pressing his face to her neck. "Your perfume drives me crazy," he whispered as he inhaled deep. "You smell so damn good." Then his mouth opened up wide on her throat. "But you taste even better."

And then his lips moved to hers and he was kissing her again, his mouth working over hers as one of his hands went to the apex of her thighs. He ran his fingers up her center, pressing into the lace.

Abby shifted forward, moving her hands from behind her and grabbing on to Logan's shirt. She fisted the material in her hands and tugged it out of his gray slacks. She was working the buttons a moment later, but her impatience got the best of her and she ripped it open.

He grinned against her mouth as buttons scattered across the wooden floor, but he didn't break the kiss. She ran her hands across his shoulders, slipping beneath the fabric and pushing the shirt down his arms. His hands moved from her body for just a moment as he dropped his arms and his shirt fell to the floor.

She pulled back from the kiss as her hands traveled down his chest, her fingers moving over his muscles. It wasn't like she hadn't seen him without his shirt on before. She'd been in and out of the locker room over the past three months after all, but she'd never allowed herself to appreciate everything that his body had to offer. She couldn't. It had been hands off.

Until now.

He was...there were no words to accurately describe him. He was one hundred and ninety-five pounds of male perfection.

Her fingertips followed the trail of hair that ran down his abs and disappeared below the waistband of his slacks. She reached for the button before she started to work his zipper down.

Now this was a part of his anatomy that she'd never seen before, and she found herself holding her breath as she pushed his slacks down his hips, exposing him to her more than eager gaze.

Why was she not surprised that Logan was going commando?

His now freed erection immediately sprang up, and she reached out, wrapping her hand around it and stroking him from base to tip.

"Well, aren't you impressive?" she whispered.

"Flattery will get you everywhere." He reached up and touched her chin, pushing gently until he could cover her mouth with his. His tongue dipped in, finding hers, moving in slow delicious thrusts that had her body craving more.

So much more.

"Bed," she said against his mouth.

"Yes, ma'am." He moved back just a little as he freed his legs from his pants. She only had a second to admire him in all his naked glory before he stepped forward and grabbed her.

She gasped, startled as his hands gripped her waist and he pulled her up off the table. Her legs automatically wrapped around his hips as he carried her through the cabin.

* * *

Logan was pretty sure nothing had ever felt better than when he slid inside of Abby's body. Her back arched off the bed and she clutched at his shoulders, her nails biting into his skin.

He buried his face in her neck as he stilled, letting her adjust around him before he started to move. He also took the moment to try to get a little bit of control over himself.

He'd be lying if he said he hadn't imagined what this would be like for months now, and his imagination was nothing close to the reality.

Abby was perfection. The whole damn package.

The thing was, she wasn't his typical package. He liked tall, leggy blondes. Abby Fields was none of those things.

She was better.

He pulled back and looked down into those bright blue eyes of hers, eyes that he hadn't been able to get out of his head since he'd first seen her. He ran one of his hands up her side, tracing those curves that filled out those skirts she loved to wear, and to her breasts that were more than a generous handful. He knew this from personal experience as he'd now had them in his hands tonight.

She had a pretty remarkable hourglass figure, if he did say so himself.

And he did.

But those weren't his mission at the moment. No, he wanted his hands in her hair. She always wore it pinned up, not a strand out of place. Well, it was more than ruffled now; the red strands were spread out across the pillows in a glorious mess.

She pulled her legs up and wrapped them around his waist, her bare feet pressing into his lower back. He lowered his mouth to hers, needing to taste her on his tongue as he began to move his hips. Pulling out before he'd slowly sink back in.

He'd been foolish to try to resist this, try to resist her. He'd been fighting a losing battle. Actually no, that wasn't true.

He'd finally won.

"Oh God, Logan." Abby pulled back and moaned his name, long and low, her limbs tightening around him as she started to move, seeking more friction. "Harder. *Please!*"

Well, she was just full of surprises tonight. And who was he to deny her what they both clearly wanted.

He grabbed her hands, his fingers locking with hers as he pinned them to the bed above their heads.

"This okay?" he asked.

She nodded, licking her lips as she continued to move her hips.

"Perfect," he said as he thrust inside of her.

Her eyes closed as her entire body arched up and she pressed her head back into the pillow. He pulled out before he pushed back in, harder just like she wanted. He wasn't sure how long they moved like that, wasn't sure how long he was lost in her, before her hands tightened in his and she was no longer moaning his name.

Nope, she was screaming it. She lost it beneath him, her body tightening around his and setting off his own chain of events.

Logan buried his face in Abby's neck, inhaling the scent of her as he caught his breath. When he pulled back a moment later, she gave him a sleepy smile.

"I'll be right back." He kissed her mouth before he reluctantly pulled from her body and went to the bathroom.

When he stepped back into the room a couple of minutes later, it was to find Abby sitting up in bed. The sheet was wrapped around her chest, and her auburn hair was sticking out like a messy halo.

He looked at her scattered garments on the floor. The thigh-high stockings that he'd peeled her out of with his teeth, her lace underwear, and those damn red shoes.

There were little bows on the backs and they'd been driving Logan out of his fucking mind all night. But she always wore heels, so they therefore always drove him out of his fucking mind.

She always drove him out of his fucking mind.

His eyes came up and focused on her as she shifted, her naked legs moving against the sheets. It was that awkward moment after of *do I stay, or do I go?*

He wanted her to stay.

"So this cabin gets a little drafty at night."

Her mouth quirked to the side. "That so?"

"Yeah." He crossed the room to the bed, placing both of his hands on either side of her. "So in an effort to conserve body heat, you should sleep in here."

"Smart." She nodded, running her hand up his bare chest.

"Besides," he said as he leaned forward, gently pushing her back down onto the bed. He followed, hovering over her as he pressed his mouth to hers. "I'm not even remotely finished with you."

Chapter 2

A Valentine's Day Hangover

A repetitive buzzing was going off near Abby's head. She buried her head farther in the pillow and tried to ignore it. She didn't want to get up. She wanted to go back to sleep and return to the dream she'd been having.

God it had been good. Filled with kissing and moaning and the hottest man she'd ever encountered in her life.

Yeah, she wanted more of that.

A lot more of that.

But the buzzing wasn't stopping. She shifted and reached up, her body stretching with the movement. It was then that her legs brushed up against somebody else's and a hand came up to her hip, skimming over her skin before it went flat on her belly and pulled her entire body back.

Not a dream.

Nope.

She'd actually done it. Actually slept with Logan James, and now she was spooning with him.

"Someone keeps calling you," he said before he pressed his mouth to her neck. His low sexy voice moved across her skin, traveling down her spine and making her shiver. She'd always thought his subtle southern drawl was incredibly sexy, but good God how was a girl supposed to react to it first thing in the morning?

She grabbed the phone and looked at the screen. She had five missed calls from her more than somewhat overeager assistant Brooke.

"It's work. It's probably about our flight."

She glanced at the alarm clock to see that it was just after seven in the morning. She should've been up an hour ago to start dealing with their new arrangements on how they were going to get to Mirabelle, Florida.

Almost four years ago, Abby's best friend Paige moved to the teeny tiny town. It hadn't been a move that Paige had been thrilled about in the beginning, but once she'd met Brendan King—her now very hot mechanic husband—she'd changed her mind on southern living.

The fact that Abby now lived only three hours away was something that both women were beyond grateful for. And it wasn't just Paige that Abby was eager to visit. She'd developed relationships with Paige's new group of friends, and she adored them all. One of them being Melanie Hart, a math teacher at the local school and the reason behind today's mission.

Dale Rigels had recently been diagnosed with cancer. Not only was he one of Mel's students, but he was her little brother Hamilton's best friend.

Dale hadn't had the easiest life. A few years ago, his father had been killed by a roadside bomb in Afghanistan. The kid had fallen on the wrong side of things after that, getting involved with a bad group of boys who liked to get high and drink. Mel's husband Bennett Hart had taken Dale under his wing, and with the help of Hamilton, they'd gotten him back on track.

But life liked to throw curve balls.

Doctors found the cancerous brain tumor four months ago. The surgery was scheduled immediately, and though they'd removed most of it, they were now pumping his body with chemicals to make sure they got the rest.

A couple weeks ago, Mel had asked Abby to set up a possible visit with Logan. Dale was having a tough time with the treatment, and they hoped that a visit from one of his heroes would lift his spirits. And it just so happened to work out that Logan would be able to make it to Dale's seventeenth birthday party.

The Stampede had been traveling for a week of away games, finishing up their last in Nashville the day before. When the Stampede headed home for Jacksonville, Abby and Logan scheduled a separate plane directly to Tallahassee, where they were going to make the hour drive down to Mirabelle. That was until the ice storm hit, canceling all flights coming in and out of the Nashville international airport.

And that was how Abby ended up in Logan's cabin in the middle of the woods of Tennessee. Ending up in his bed had been a different story...one that involved a bottle of Jack Daniel's and giving in to something she'd wanted for months now.

Him.

But in the light of day the consequences of their actions became a reality.

Logan was a client.

Not only had she never—and she meant ever—mixed business with pleasure, but there was a strict no fraternization policy for anyone working for or with the Jacksonville Stampede.

What the hell had she been thinking?

Logan shifted behind her, his hard—perfectly muscled—naked body moving against hers.

Oh right, she hadn't been thinking.

Abby pulled out of Logan's embrace and got out of bed before she headed for the bathroom, telling herself that if he wasn't touching her she might be able to think straight.

* * *

Logan had hoped for another round in bed with Abby, but as she'd been on the phone hammering out their travel plans, no such luck.

His second disappointment of the morning had been showering alone. They'd needed to get ready and head back to the airport, so showering together wasn't a possibility.

The third was her keeping a pretty good distance from him since she'd pulled away that morning and gotten out of bed. He had absolutely no regrets about the night before. Apparently that wasn't the case for her.

And he was going to get to the bottom of it real quick.

"So what's your plan, Red? You just going to act like last night didn't happen?" he asked as he loaded their bags into the trunk of the rental car before he turned to her.

"No, I don't think that's possible." A blush crept up the little exposed area of her neck and to her cheeks. "But it—"

"Don't say it was a mistake." He didn't take his eyes off her as he reached up and closed the trunk.

"I wasn't going to." She took a deep breath before she let it out. It was cold outside and her breath hung in the air between them. "I was going to say it can't happen again."

"It can't?" he asked slowly. "Well that's disappointing."

"Logan, I—"

"No," he cut her off again. "No need to explain."

He got it. He did the brush-off all the time. He'd done it well and he'd done it often. But he hadn't been finished with Abby.

He'd be lying if he said he wasn't more than a little frustrated with her change of heart. He'd been resisting her for what felt like forever now, and he would've liked a little bit more time enjoying all of what she had to offer.

And damn did she have a lot to offer.

It had been a while since he'd been able to get that lost in a woman. Really he was pretty sure he'd *never* gotten that lost in a woman, and it had been about way more than just her body. He'd been looking forward to exploring whatever that *more* was in detail.

Well, he was just going to have to get over that little pipe dream now, wasn't he?

And he was doing okay until they got into the airplane and he was sitting right next to her. Closed confined spaces and the smell of Abby's perfume didn't mix very well with his mental state. It made him think about what it had been like kissing her, what it had been like moving inside of her.

He didn't get his fascination with her, either. He was around beautiful women all the time, and none of them was as complicated as the one next to him.

It was more than somewhat baffling to the mind that something so tiny could be the biggest pain in his ass.

He didn't get it. He *truly* didn't get it.

When he was out on the ice, he was dealing with other hockey players who were two hundred and ten pounds of amped-up male and wouldn't even hesitate to smash his face into the boards. So one would think he could handle the pint-sized redhead.

But if Abby Fields was anything, it was determined. Where many of the publicists didn't bother asking Logan to do anything anymore, she was new and hadn't given up yet. After three months, her insistence hadn't lessened at all, and he had a feeling it never would with her. He just got that vibe.

He'd been more than resistant to work with the Stampede PR department over the years. He was absolutely fine being in the spotlight when he was out on the ice, but off the ice? No.

He wasn't one for being exploited. He was a firm believer that his personal life should be private. He saw it all the time, guys going on reality TV shows, having cameras in their faces for twenty-four hours a day. He watched as some offhand comment cost them the respect of fans and their divorces got played out in the tabloids.

He was pretty sure that no one's life could hold up under the scrutiny of being entirely in the public eye. People made mistakes, and some pretty big ones at that. He wasn't taking the risk with his privacy.

It just wasn't for him, and he said "no" about 90 percent of the time. But there were certain things he just couldn't say no to. What they were doing today was definitely one of them.

It had been eight years since his daughter's death. Eight years since he'd held Madison in his arms, since he'd felt her arms wrapped around his neck, since he'd heard her sweet little giggle bubble out of her mouth.

If there'd been anything that could've been done for his daughter, anything that would've given her just a little bit of joy in her last days, and somebody hadn't done it for her? Yeah, he wouldn't have gotten over that.

Not that he'd gotten over anything that had to do with Madison's death. She'd left this world just after her fifth birthday. She'd been gone longer than she'd even been here.

It still hurt like hell.

It would *always* hurt like hell.

And just like his daughter, the kid they were going to visit only had one parent by his side.

Logan met Cassidy Thomas during his freshman year at the University of Michigan. They'd only been dating for two months when she told him she was pregnant. He still considered it a miracle that she actually went through with the pregnancy. But he was pretty sure that had more to do with her God-fearing mother than anything else, not that Lana Thomas ever was all that involved with her granddaughter, either.

Cassidy bailed after Madison's diagnosis, but she'd never really wanted anything to do with her daughter in the first place. The pregnancy had been an accident, and Cassidy made sure to remind Logan of that fact often.

How a mother could walk out on her dying child he did not know, but Madison had been better off. And it wasn't like she'd been alone. Logan's parents, brother, and sister had all been there, had all loved her.

His family did everything they could for his daughter, no questions asked. So stranger or not, he could return the favor for someone else's kid, no matter how hard it was.

At least they weren't going to a hospital. Those visits were the hardest for him because they always brought him back to Madison's last days.

He shook his head trying to pull himself out of the past. Abby shifted next to him, and he caught the smell of her perfume again.

Fantastic.

He grabbed his headphones, sticking the buds into his ears and settling in for what promised to be a long-ass flight.

* * *

Abby stood on the edge of the room, sipping her hot coffee and trying to look at anything and everything besides Logan. There was enough going on to keep her somewhat distracted.

The room was filled with people, Dale's family and friends taking up the limited space in Virginia Rigels's living room.

"Dale's father always loved hockey," Virginia said as she came to stand next to Abby. She was a very pretty woman, small and curvy with dark brown hair and a certain amount of exhaustion behind her hazel eyes.

"Vince was from Minnesota. Grew up playing the game. But then he joined the Marines and spent the last part of his life in the desert." A sad smile turned up her mouth. "He missed the ice. He'd watch games with Dale when he was home."

"Mel told me that Mr. Rigels was a huge Stampede fan."

"He was. They were his team as soon as he moved to Florida. He was a fan of Mr. James pretty much the instant he was traded to the team. Whenever Vince was stationed overseas, Dale would write him letters with blow-by-blow accounts of the games. That was their thing. I wish Vince could see what the team was doing this year."

To say that the Stampede was having a good season would be an understatement. It was the middle of February and not only was the team forty-two and fourteen, but it was currently on an eight-game winning streak.

The players were doing phenomenally, including Logan. For

the last two years he'd been ranked in the top ten players in the league for assists. Jace Kilpatrick, another forward on Logan's line, was ranked as a top scorer. The Stampede's captain, Andre Fabian, was the third on the line, and when the three of them were out on the ice they dominated.

It was something to see the three men working together. It was like they read each other's minds, anticipating moves with a skilled accuracy before they were even made.

"I can't thank you enough for setting this up with Melanie," Virginia said, reaching out and putting her hand on Abby's arm. "This means the world to Dale...and to me."

"It was no problem." Abby reached out and covered Virginia's hand with her own. "As soon as I told Logan about it, he said yes." Though this was something she still didn't quite understand.

She was used to hearing "no" from him. Sometimes she wouldn't even get her entire proposal out before he'd shake his head.

His words from the other day echoed in her head quite clearly.

"Look, I don't like my personal life being exploited for the public. Just because some people know who I am because I play hockey doesn't mean they deserve to know what I ate for dinner, or if I prefer boxers or briefs, or the last woman I took to bed."

Well, today she knew the answers to all three of those questions: filet mignon and asparagus with hollandaise sauce; neither as he liked to go commando; and her.

Not that she'd be reporting any of that information to anyone. In fact, this entire visit to Mirabelle was off limits for PR endeavors. Logan had made a point about it. He'd said he'd be more than happy to do it, but Dale and his family were in no way to be exploited.

Logan didn't care who the kid told, or what photos he wanted to share on whatever forms of social media he used. The Stampede were just off limits to use them.

"If it comes out in other ways, so be it," he'd said, and shrugged when she'd gotten him to agree to it weeks ago. *"But I'm not using his sickness to make myself look good."*

He was honorable, that was for sure. And a whole host of other things. She liked him way more than what was professionally acceptable.

Well, the night before had proved that. Proved it in spades.

Abby shook her head and tried to focus on the woman next to her as opposed to the man across the room. But Virginia didn't let her.

"I'm pretty sure he's never going to take that jersey off." She nodded at the group of men. "Or that beanie." She beamed as she squeezed Abby's arm. She let go and excused herself, going over to her son.

Logan had brought the kid enough Stampede merchandise to keep him clothed for a good long while. Hats, T-shirts, sweatshirts, and then there were the hockey pucks, one of Logan's personal hockey sticks—the list went on and on. The knit hat that Dale was currently sporting was black with the team mascot Pete the Elephant on the front. Logan had been wearing it, but the second he met Dale he'd quickly pulled it off his head and placed it on Dale's bald one.

A cold front had settled in over the South and it was averaging below freezing. Abby had dealt with her fair share of chilly weather when she lived in Philadelphia and Washington, D.C., and they might not be dealing with snow, but it was still pretty cold. She had no doubt that Dale was feeling it.

But the kid was all smiles at the moment. He and his best

friend Hamilton—who was on the other side of Dale, a brand-new Stampede ball cap of his own pulled backward on his head—were sitting at the dining room table with Logan, and the group of men that had been aptly dubbed the *Men of Mirabelle*.

Mel's husband Bennett was sitting on the other side of Dale. He was both a mentor and a bit of a big brother to the kid. Paige's husband Brendan was next, followed by her brother-in-law Jaxson Anderson. Nathanial Shepherd, more commonly referred to as Shep, was also at the table. He was the local bartender and he had a close relationship with both Dale and Hamilton; the boys had been helping on the remodel of the inn that Shep and his wife Hannah lived in.

The plan, before Logan and Abby had gotten delayed in Tennessee, was for Logan to stay in one of the completed rooms at the inn. If that had happened, Abby wouldn't have slept with him, because she'd planned to stay the night with Brendan and Paige.

She didn't regret her decisions from the night before. She'd given in to something she wanted. But how did the saying go? Too much of a good thing is a bad thing.

So it didn't matter how good what you wanted looked with his shirt off, or if you hadn't been given enough time to map his muscles out with your fingers, or explore the tattooed M on his left shoulder blade.

She guessed it was the University of Michigan M as that was his alma mater and he'd played on the hockey team for all four years of college. Except his was filled in with black ink. She hadn't really gotten to see him from behind—a damn shame really—so she didn't know any more than that.

But maybe that was a good thing.

Overindulgence could lead to disastrous consequences, and

Abby had a feeling that Logan would be worse than the effects a pint of Ben & Jerry's ice cream would have on her thighs.

But it was beginning to become difficult for her to hold strong with her decision, because every time he laughed she'd feel that flutter low in her belly. Actually, it wasn't a flutter anymore. It was a full-on tidal wave.

"I've seen that look before."

Abby turned to the side just as her best friend Paige walked up, balancing her son Trevor on her hip. The toddler would be two at the end of May, and he was speaking up a storm these days. He was the perfect blend of mother and father, with Paige's dark brown hair and Brendan's light blue eyes.

"*Ab-we!*" He leaned to the side and reached for her. She complied with his demands immediately, putting down her cup of coffee before lifting him from Paige's arms and settling him on her side. He rested his face in the crook of her neck, content with his new location.

"He's tired. Too much excitement for the day."

"I wish I could take a nap, too," Abby said as she began to rub his back soothingly. "And what look are you talking about?"

"The one you keep giving your hockey player."

Abby's hand faltered for just a moment. "He isn't *my* hockey player."

"But you admit to the look?"

"What look?" she asked again.

"One of unadulterated lust."

She bit her lip as she turned and looked up at her best friend. Five-inch black pumps or not, Abby had and would forever be shorter than Paige. Paige was five-foot-ten and like Abby had a certain obsession with tall shoes. She was sporting a pair of knee-high leather boots today that gave her an added four inches.

Abby had never been able to withhold the truth from Paige. *Ever.* They'd been best friends since they were five years old, and a bond over puffy Cheetos in their pretty pink *Little Mermaid* lunch boxes was one that couldn't be broken.

They'd been through a lot together over the last twenty-four years, both of them losing their fathers. Though in entirely different ways. Paige's father, Trevor Morrison, died almost three years ago. The aggressive form of pancreatic cancer never even gave him a chance. He'd been the best kind of man and the best kind of father, and he'd pretty much been Abby's since she was ten years old.

Jim Fields walked out on Abby and her mother and didn't even look back. Abby had seen him sporadically over the last nineteen years, and every visit was somehow even more demoralizing than the last. She'd never met a more indifferent man.

Abby had her fair share of daddy issues and they'd all spilled over to her failed romances, of which there'd been quite a few.

"Something…uh…happened last night," Abby whispered.

"What kind of something?"

"A naked kind of something."

Paige's eyes got huge. "Seriously?"

Abby just nodded.

"Holy crap, woman. Good thing you're staying the night, otherwise I'd be forced to follow your butt to Jacksonville to get the whole story. I knew something was up; you've been on edge all afternoon."

"I'll be fine when he's on his merry way out of Mirabelle. I can't think straight when he's in the same room."

"How's that going to pan out when you have to work with him?" Paige asked seriously.

"I don't know." It was something Abby had been thinking

about all day, especially after her very short conversation with Logan that morning. He'd barely talked to her since she'd told him it wasn't going to happen again.

Well, he being all taciturn with her was at least one thing that was back to normal.

She couldn't help letting her gaze wander over to the table with the guys, nor could she stop her eyes from focusing on Logan. He reached up and scratched the back of his neck, the move causing his arm to flex. Then he moved his palm up, running his fingers through his hair and causing some of the strands to stand up in a carelessly rumpled look.

He was too damn sexy for his own good. She hadn't been this attracted to a man in well…ever. And if there'd been any thought in the back of her mind about "getting him out of her system" after one night, she'd been *horribly* mistaken. If anything, she just wanted him more.

Why had she said it couldn't happen again?

It was at that moment that he looked up, his eyes landing on hers. She didn't even take a second to register what she found in those mesmerizing green-gold depths before she pulled her gaze away.

"I…uh…can you take him?" Abby quickly handed Trevor off to Paige, not making eye contact with her friend before she made a beeline outside. She needed some fresh air.

She was just hot. That was why her palms were sweating and the scarf around her neck was suddenly suffocating. Yeah, it had absolutely nothing to do with the man she'd just run away from.

Chapter 3

The Power of Peppermint Schnapps

Logan was pretty sure Abby couldn't have gotten out of the building faster if her pants were on fire. He was actually amazed with how quickly she'd moved, considering the heels she was wearing that day.

Yet another pair that were guaranteed to drive him out of his fucking skull.

He'd been doing a good job of not focusing on her for the last couple of hours. It wasn't so much the "out of sight, out of mind" thing as much as he was being thoroughly entertained by the crowd around him.

Dale and his best friend Hamilton were a regular little pair of comedians. Logan was beyond impressed with Dale. The kid was ridiculously positive, and given the hand he'd been dealt both with the cancer and losing his father a few years ago, it would've been easy to fall into the anger and depression. Something Logan knew full well as he'd fallen into them himself.

But the community Dale had here was awesome; the group of

guys around the table a shining example of how real men lived good lives. Lives that weren't in front of a camera and dissected every single minute.

Sure, everybody had difficult things they had to deal with, but he imagined it might be just a little bit simpler if it all wasn't in the eye of the public. And part of him longed for that.

He'd been burned more than once; it was one of the reasons he tried to keep his personal life private. His relationships weren't any business of the public anyway, and really they were few and far between. It was hard to date considering the fact that he'd been pretty numb for almost the last decade.

But he hadn't felt numb this morning...hadn't felt numb when he'd woken up with Abby in his bed. Though, he was pretty sure he hadn't ever been numb around her. She had made him hot under the collar for months now.

He noticed her the very first time he saw her, and she managed to always draw his attention whenever she was in the same room. She sparked an interest in him that he hadn't felt in what seemed like forever.

He tried his damnedest to ignore it. To ignore her.

But he was beyond ignoring it now, especially after knowing what it was like to be set on fire.

Logan excused himself from the table, heading for the doors that Abby had just fled out of moments before. When he stepped outside, she turned at the noise and looked over at him.

Her shoulders immediately straightened and she took a deep breath.

"Things should be wrapping up soon. Then you can be on your way home," she said as she rubbed her hands up and down her arms.

He had a feeling the gesture was more needing something to do than actually being cold.

"You already want me out of here?" he asked as he walked up next to her, leaning against the railing of the porch and looking out at the view. The Rigels's house was built on stilts by a river, the dark waters rushing behind it.

"I just figured you'd want to get home and back to normal."

"You have no idea what I want, Red."

Her entire body tensed up more, something that he didn't even know was possible. If she got any more rigid, her spine would probably snap. It was such a contrast, this moment compared to how pliant she'd been the night before.

What he *wanted* was more of that. Her beneath him...or on top. He wasn't all that picky.

He turned to her, and she automatically moved in response, looking up at him. He reached out slowly, running his fingers down the side of her face and to her chin where he lightly pushed up.

When she didn't pull away he lowered his mouth to hers, just a soft kiss to her lips. Her mouth opened on a sigh and her entire body seemed to relax into his. He took that as his cue and his other hand came up, sliding around her hip and to her lower back. He pulled her fully into his body as he slipped his tongue passed her lips.

"I've been craving that since I woke up this morning," he whispered against her mouth before he dove back in.

This time her hands came up and were in his hair, her fingers trailing down the back of his neck. Holy hell she made him hard in an instant. As she was flush up against him, he was pretty sure she was fully aware of it, too.

He pulled away from her just enough to where he could look down into her face. Her eyes opened slowly, those startling blues more than a little bit dazed.

"I take it back," he said as he ran his thumb across her lips. "I do want to know why last night can't happen again."

Within a matter of seconds, Abby managed to get ahold of herself. His words bringing her back to reality. She dropped her hands from the back of his neck and reached for his wrists, pulling his hand from her face and the other from her lower back.

"We work together." She took a step away from him, and despite her best efforts at composure, her breathing was still erratic.

"All right, I promise to be just as uncooperative as I was before. No one will suspect a thing."

The side of her mouth twitched and he knew she was fighting a smile. "It's more complicated than that."

"How is it more complicated?"

"There's a no fraternization policy with the Stampede."

"What? There's nothing like that in my contract."

"No." She shook her head. "There isn't. But it's in mine."

"Seriously?"

"Yes."

"Stupidest thing I've ever heard." He shrugged his shoulders. "Truth: I want you, Red. It's as simple as that. And I don't think a piece of paper—"

"It's not just a piece of paper," she cut him off. "And it's not simple. This is my job. *Your* job isn't threatened by us fooling around."

He hadn't labeled what he and Abby had done, but it sure as shit hadn't been fooling around. That was for rink bunnies, guys on the team who forgot the names of their dates the next day. He'd dabbled in it over the years, picking up a girl here or there, but that was more about scratching an itch.

Which wasn't something he equated with Abby. She was... more than that. He had no fucking clue *what* she was. But he'd really like to find out.

She apparently didn't.

"Then why weren't you thinking about that last night?" he asked.

"I...I don't know, Logan. I wasn't thinking about a lot of things last night. Being alone with you like that, away from everyone and everything, I guess I just took a break from reality."

He nodded as he looked at her. "Well, I think you should go back to that. No good ever came from overthinking something." He took a step forward, his hands going to her hips as he leaned down and pressed his mouth to hers one more time. "We aren't back home yet. We still have one more night before we have to go back to *reality*." He definitely wanted more than one night, but he got the sense that he was just going to have to take this one step at a time.

"Wh-what?" she asked, dazed.

"I'm not going home tonight. Shep invited me to stay. I can still get my night at the inn. Plus, he wanted to show me his bar and the brewery."

"You're staying?" Her eyes narrowed, attempting to focus on his face and his words.

"Yup. I don't have practice until Tuesday afternoon, so you aren't getting rid of me yet, Red. And in the honor of our game last night, I'll keep up with the truth," he whispered as he leaned in close to her ear. "After being inside you, I don't know that I'll ever return to reality. I'd like to explore this whole thing further."

"Further?" The word fell from her mouth slowly, like she was sounding it out.

"Yes, further. It needs to be a secret? That's fine with me. You know I don't like my private life to be out in the public. And to be quite honest, the things I want to do when you're around aren't all that appropriate for the public eye, so it works for me. You just need to figure out if it works for you."

The door behind them opened and Logan's hands fell away from Abby's body. He turned to see Mrs. Rigels sticking her head outside.

"Dale is about to take a nap. I think he's had about as much excitement as he can handle for the day."

"I'll just say goodbye," Logan said, heading for the door. "And finalize our plans for tomorrow."

"Okay," Virginia nodded before she headed back in.

"Plans for tomorrow?" Abby asked, following him across the deck.

"I'm eating breakfast with Dale and Hamilton in the morning. Apparently it's imperative that I get a chocolate chip muffin at Café Lula."

He held the door open for her as they stepped inside, and she looked at him as she passed by, her confusion evident by her furrowed eyebrows.

"And then we can head back to *reality* together," he finished.

And just like that Abby's look of confusion was replaced with frustration, her brows suddenly slanting down and those lips of hers bunching together.

Well, she could just join the club.

* * *

"All right woman, spill," Paige demanded as she took a sip of hot chocolate from the mug she clutched in her hands.

They were sitting on opposite ends of the couch, their backs resting against the arms and their legs stretched out toward the middle. Abby had changed into a pair of jeans and a sweater when they'd gotten back to Paige and Brendan's house. The fire burning in front of them was keeping her nice and toasty along with her cup of hot chocolate, topped with schnapps and whipped cream.

Brendan was in the kitchen putting something together for dinner and Trevor was taking a nap, still completely tuckered out from the day's events.

"I don't even know where to start," Abby said, lifting her mug to her lips and taking a good mouthful. She wasn't sure what warmed her more, the temperature of the liquid or the burn from the alcohol. "Holy crap, how much schnapps did you put in here?"

"I don't know"—Paige shrugged—"I just eyeballed it."

Well, this would be the second time in less than twenty-four hours that a little bit of alcohol was going to give her some loose lips. Though, she would've told Paige everything anyway. She always told her everything.

So Abby took a deep breath and just dove right on in from the beginning, from the first time she saw Logan James and knew she was in trouble, all the way through their conversations and how his resistance made her want to throttle him.

"Oh, my gosh," Paige spluttered on her hot chocolate when Abby got to the part where he put the bottle of whiskey on the table and explained the rules of *Strip, Shoot, or Truth*. Though, the rules had pretty much been self-explanatory. "I can't believe you played a drinking game with him that involved stripping." Paige's eyes were round as she stared across at Abby in wonder.

"It just…happened." Abby shrugged as she started chewing on her lip.

"How does something like that just happen?" Paige's eyebrows climbed up her forehead. "One second you're talking about the weather and the next you're showing him the color of your panties?"

"There were a few steps in between."

"I'll just bet there were." Paige grinned. "Please continue." She waved her hand in the air.

"I think you're enjoying this a little too much."

"Um, excuse me. I believe you were more than a little relentless getting information when it came to Brendan and me."

"Yes, but he was your prince charming—"

"Damn right I was," Brendan called out from the kitchen.

Abby really didn't mind having this conversation with Brendan in earshot; if anything he'd become like a brother to her in the last couple of years. Besides, she kind of wanted his opinion on the whole thing as well.

"So was he any good?" Paige waggled her eyebrows as her grin overtook her face. "Who am I kidding? I've seen that man in person now. Of course he was good."

A loud clatter came from the kitchen. It sounded like a pot being dropped on the tile floor. A second later Brendan's head popped out from around the opening.

"You best tread lightly there, woman."

"Oh baby, you know I only have eyes for you." Paige batted her eyes at him as she kissed the air. He shook his head and disappeared back into the kitchen. "So on a scale of one to ten, compared to your past experiences with one being AJ Clifford and ten being Cameron Spruce, where does Logan measure up?"

"Paige, he sets a new scale. Cameron would be a six, six and a half, and Logan would be a thirty."

"Why the hell are you sitting across from me right now and not in that man's bed?" Paige asked, completely deadpan.

"Be serious for a second." Abby nudged Paige's foot with her own.

"I am! I've never seen you run from anything before. You

practically sprinted away from him earlier today. What was up with that?"

"I can't think straight when he's around."

"No kidding."

Abby finished the last of her drink and set it down on the table next to her. She studied the empty mug for a second, a nice little buzz calming down her spinning brain.

"He...um...he said something to me before we left the Rigels's house," she said as she focused on Paige again.

"About?"

"Spending another night with him...well, spending many nights with him actually. He wants to...explore this whole thing between us."

"And you don't? Holy crap, Abby, he wants to explore it? What are you waiting for?"

"It isn't a game of Marco Polo, Paige. It's complicated."

"Sex is always complicated. But when it's good and involves men like Logan James, one should explore the hell out of it. I'm going to repeat my earlier question: why aren't you in that man's bed?"

"Really? This from the girl who took months to get into Brendan's bed?" Abby countered.

"Yes, but once I was *in* it, I didn't *leave* it."

"Damn right you didn't," Brendan called out again.

Paige rolled her eyes but the grin spread across her face counteracted the gesture. There was something about seeing Paige and Brendan together that gave Abby more than a little bit of hope when it came to love. It was something she'd lacked drastically after her father's departure. And there was no small amount of pleasure that filled her at seeing her best friend so happy with the love of her life.

Though she wasn't sure if that was her dormant maudlin sentimentality or the heat spreading throughout her limbs from the remainder of the drink she'd just downed.

"Seriously, how much schnapps did you put in there?" Abby asked, pointing to her empty cup. "Are you not feeling it?"

"Uhhh, no." Paige's cheeks turned a bright pink as she shook her head. "Mine was a virgin."

"What? Why? Did Brendan knock you up again?"

"Yeah." The smile that had been on Paige's face moments before was nothing, *nothing*, to the one that was now on her face. She was beaming brighter than Abby had ever seen before.

"Seriously?" Abby couldn't help reflecting the sheer joy radiating from her friend.

"Damn right I did." There was no small amount of pride in Brendan's voice.

"Why didn't you tell me earlier?" She grabbed a pillow and lightly smacked Paige's legs with it.

"Because we were discussing you. We were going to get there eventually."

"Agh!" Abby moved across the couch to sit next to her best friend. The two women embraced, holding on to each other for a good long while. "I'm so happy for you," Abby said as she pulled back. There were tears in both of their eyes. "When did you find out?"

"I just took the test last week." Paige reached up and wiped at her eyes. "My mom and Brendan's grandmother know, but we aren't telling anyone else until we get past the first trimester."

"Planned?"

"Yeah." Paige nodded.

"When are you due?" Abby asked as she moved back to her end of the sofa and settled in among the pillows.

"October."

"New Year's resolution?"

"Something like that."

"Story for later?" Abby didn't hesitate to keep up with her line of questioning.

"Hmmm, I think so. Because we need to focus on your current situation."

Abby let out an exasperated sigh. "There isn't anything to focus on. It can't go any further." She grabbed a pillow and pulled it into her lap, tracing the pattern as opposed to looking at Paige.

"Why the hell not?" Paige asked as she nudged Abby's foot with her own.

Abby looked up and took another deep breath. She let it out slowly before she spoke. "You know why not. I'm putting my career at risk, *my* reputation. And for what? Sex? I've never been this reckless before."

"I think there's something to be said for that."

"What? That when I'm around him I lose all of my sense along with my clothes?"

"I was going to say that you really like him, but what you said works, too."

"Ugh, Paige, what am I going to do?" She buried her head in the pillow and groaned.

"Not hide," Paige said as she nudged Abby's feet again.

Abby pulled her head from the pillow and focused on her friend. "Why not? Wouldn't that be easier?"

"Because hiding isn't like you. And I've never known you to go for the easy route. Case in point, the first guy that's really caught your attention in years is for all intents and purposes off limits."

"I was doing just fine until I realized he was interested, too."

"And why wouldn't he be? Hello, you're Abby Freaking Fields. Publicist extraordinaire. You're amazing, brilliant, beautiful, and kind. Plus you have fabulous taste in shoes."

"I need to come visit you more often. You give a girl a serious boost to her confidence," Abby said as she fluffed her hair and preened.

"I'm being serious!"

"So am I!" Abby laughed.

"Brendan!" Paige called out. Her husband appeared in the doorway a second later, drying his hands on a towel. "What do you think, babe?"

He tossed the towel onto his shoulder as he leaned against the jamb and looked at them. "I've always liked Logan as an athlete. He keeps his head down and doesn't make an ass out of himself. He has no patience for the paparazzi, but to be honest, I don't think that I would, either, if there was a camera constantly in my face." He shrugged his shoulders.

"But after meeting him, talking to him," Brendan continued, "I think that he's a pretty cool guy. He came over here to see Dale with no benefit to himself. The fact that he didn't turn it into the *Logan Show* is impressive, and something you don't see all that often. He made it about the kid and not even remotely about himself. That right there says that he's a man of integrity."

"He is that." Abby agreed.

It was a fact that the man had been difficult to deal with, but that didn't mean he didn't have standards. It was something she wished more people knew about him. It wasn't about exploiting him—at least it hadn't been for her, she wasn't sure what he'd dealt with before she'd been hired—it was more about the public knowing there were athletes out there who were more than capable of not making asses out of themselves.

It was a feat to be sure.

"I will say this, though, if he hurts you, he's going to lose a lot more than a fan." The serious look on Brendan's face was not to be messed with, and Abby was touched by his words.

"Thank you."

"No problem." He nodded before he pushed off the wall and went back into the kitchen.

"I'm not encouraging you to do something stupid," Paige said. "Really I'm not, and if I hadn't seen you around him, met him in person, I'd tell you to tread cautiously. But there's something about him, Abby, something about the way he looks at you, that I don't think you should ignore."

Yeah, Abby was beginning to think she was at the point where she *couldn't* ignore it. She'd be lying if she said she hadn't wanted him to kiss her out on that porch. Lying if she said his hands on her body hadn't been perfection. But his touch this afternoon had been nothing to what she'd experienced last night, his palms sliding over her bare skin, his mouth on her breasts.

"You said he's intensely private, right?" Paige asked, bringing Abby out of her very dirty thoughts. "Do you think he would ever say anything about a relationship with you to the public?"

"No." Abby shook her head. "I don't think that he would."

"My question to you is this: do you want to see where this could go? If it's more than just sex?"

"Yes." Abby was shocked at how quickly the word fell from her mouth. She blamed the alcohol. And Paige. Somehow this was her best friend's fault, too.

"Okay, so what do we do now?" Paige asked.

Well, wasn't that the question of the day?

Chapter 4

Round Two . . . and Three . . . and Four

Logan sat at the bar of the Sleepy Sheep, a smorgasbord of beers laid out before him. Shep had filled up six different tasters and laid them out on the counter.

"All of these are your own brews?" Logan asked as he picked up the darkest one on the very end.

"Four of them are; the other two are local."

Shep had given Logan a tour of the brand-new brewery that had been built on the side of the bar. Two large shiny tanks were currently set up for production, but there was definitely more space to work with. Shep had plans for at least four more tanks; he just needed to make the money first.

But he was apparently well on his way because his beer was selling like crazy, and as Logan made his way through his sampler, he understood why.

"Holy shit, this stuff is phenomenal. Can I get a full glass of this one?" he asked, holding up the red in his hand.

"That's one of my favorites, too. It took me a couple of batches to get the flavors just right, so I named it after my wife." He smirked. "That's the Complicated Redhead."

"That so?" Logan asked as he eyed the remainder of the beer. Well, wasn't that interesting?

He'd met Shep's wife Hannah earlier when he arrived at the Seaside Escape Inn. She'd been more than accommodating as she'd gotten him settled into his wing of the inn. They were in the process of remodeling the three-story building into different apartments. The entire bottom floor was Shep and Hannah's house, but the other two floors had been divided into six different sections.

Two of the apartments were done, and they were quite remarkable with their massive windows looking out on the Gulf Coast. Wooden floors stretched out throughout the rooms, stunning bathrooms boasted of Jacuzzi tubs and separate walk-in showers, and an assortment of antique furniture mixed in perfectly among brand-new pieces.

Hannah went around showing the completed rooms to Logan, pointing out all the work that Dale had done. The colors he'd picked out, the tiles he'd laid, and so on.

"He's a very talented kid. And it means a lot that you came. Thank you." She'd stretched up and given Logan a kiss on the cheek before she left him to settle in.

He hadn't seen her complicated side, but he had no doubt that she'd probably given Shep a run for his money. He had a feeling if there was a drink named after Abby, it would be called the Runaway Red...or something like that. He tipped the glass back and downed the last of it.

He wondered if it was the red hair that made them so complicated...or was it the fact that they were just women in general?

He wasn't sure and he couldn't stop his brain from puzzling over that fact as he sipped on the fresh beer that Shep had poured him.

Because really, why did he care so much? His relationships over the last few years hadn't been very deep, not shocking as he was pretty hesitant to let anyone new into his life. He'd been burned bad with Cassidy and then losing Madison...unbearable.

So yeah, he didn't do serious. It made it that much easier when it ended and he moved on.

So why, *why*, wasn't he ready to move on from Abby?

* * *

Abby stared at the dark blue door in front of her for just a moment before she lifted her hand slowly, her knuckles rapping against the solid wood.

She was standing on the second floor of the Seaside Escape Inn. It was a massive building with the Gulf of Mexico stretching out behind it. She couldn't see the ocean as the sun had set hours ago, but she could hear the churning waters beyond the sand. The moon was absent and there were no stars in the sky, the storm clouds blocking everything out. Icy rain fell from the sky and she shivered, burrowing farther into her jacket.

She knew that Logan was back at the inn, as Hannah had texted Paige that he and Shep had returned twenty minutes ago. She still couldn't believe she was standing outside this door, waiting for him to open it.

She knew exactly what was going to happen when he opened said door. She might as well start unbuttoning her jeans now, really. Though, him doing it for her might be a little bit more fun.

Or a lotta bit.

Abby's entire body tensed as the handle rattled and the door opened. But the sexy grin spreading across Logan's face as he looked her up and down had all of her tension melting away into the freezing air around her. She'd be surprised if she wasn't making steam.

He looked good in his jeans and long-sleeved T-shirt. Comfortable as he stood in the doorway, a bottle of beer in his hand.

"Red?"

"I'm not quite ready to return to reality."

"That so?" he asked as he reached up, running his hand through his hair in that carelessly sexy way that very few men had ever been able to pull off with her.

He pulled it off in spades.

"That *is* so." She nodded, taking a step forward and pulling the beer from his grasp. He let go of it and used his now free hand to reach out.

"Good," he said as he ran his palm around her waist and to her back, where he pulled her into the foyer and more importantly into his body. He closed the door behind them, shutting out the cold dark night.

She tipped the bottle back, letting the cold drink wash down the last of any and all of her doubts.

"I like your hair like this," he said as he reached up and gently wound one of her curls around his finger. She'd pulled her hair down from its customary twist when she'd gotten back to Brendan and Paige's earlier that night. When the up-do had been released, her hair hung around her shoulders in loose curls.

"And these jeans are pretty fantastic." The hand at her waist was moving down. He slid it to her bottom where he squeezed lightly. "I've never seen you in anything besides business clothes."

"That's not true." She shook her head as she took another pull on the bottle of beer. "Last night you saw me in lingerie…and then nothing at all."

"You make a valid point." He pulled the beer from her hands, tipping it back and finishing it off before he put it on the table next to the door. "And now it's my turn to make my point."

And just like that Abby was pushed up against the wall of the entryway, Logan's mouth covering hers. His hands were working under the material of her sweater, warm against her skin as his fingers traced their way up to her breasts. His thumbs rasped over her nipples, and the moan that escaped her mouth couldn't be helped.

He shifted, and in that moment he made his *point* quite clear. His erection was pushing into her belly.

"You're staying the night, Red."

Not a question but she felt the need to answer anyway. "Yes."

Logan's hands dropped to her thighs and he pulled her up in one swift movement. She wrapped her legs around his waist as he carried her through the apartment. She guessed he was taking her to the bedroom; she wasn't exactly sure as her mouth was glued to his.

But she was confirmed right when he laid her down among all of the soft bedding a moment later. Her legs were still wrapped tightly around him, and as she hadn't loosened her hold on him in the slightest, he had no choice but to follow her down.

She reveled in the weight of him pushing her down into the mattress. It was freaking glorious. The only thing that would make it better would be if they were both naked. Well, she might as well start on that right now.

She grabbed at the back of his shirt, pulling at it with what might have been a little too much gusto.

"Need to get this off," she whispered against his mouth as she continued to work it. But as their bodies were wound so tightly together, it was a struggle.

And the struggle was real.

He pulled back and grinned down at her. "Overeager much?"

"You better believe it."

"Drop your legs," he said as he kissed her lips.

She did, and he pulled back, kneeling on the bed between her legs. He reached behind to his back, grabbing a fistful of his shirt and pulling it up and over his head. He threw it over his shoulder and paused for just a moment as he looked down at her. She took the opportunity to let her eyes rake over his body. Her fingers itched to touch him, but she kept her hands on the bed, waiting for his next move.

He reached for her and ran his hand down one of her thighs, past her knee and calf, to her ankle where he pulled her foot from the bed. She was wearing fur-lined moccasins and he slipped one off her foot before he held it up for her to see.

"This isn't part of your usual fanfare, either. I like seeing this side of you, Red," he said before he tossed the shoe over his shoulder and repeated the process with her other foot.

When her feet were both bare, she placed them flat on the bed, lifting her hips just slightly as she adjusted herself.

Logan licked his lips as he reached out and pushed the hem of her sweater up, exposing her lower belly. He ran his fingers across her bare skin, tracing around her belly button before he dipped lower to the top of her jeans.

He unsnapped the button before he lowered the zipper. She raised her hips as he grabbed the top of her jeans and shimmied them down her legs. They were on the floor in a matter of seconds.

"God," he groaned as he stared at her panties. There was just a scrap of cloth in the front, and then three strings on each side ran around her hips and to the back.

Before Abby had the chance to say or do anything, Logan was lowering himself onto the bed, pushing her thighs apart with his shoulders.

He kissed the very top of her panties before he trailed his lips down. Then he opened his mouth on her, finding her clit with his tongue through the fabric.

Her eyes closed and she melted back into the bed, giving in to the sensations of his mouth working her over. Her hands came up, her fingers running through his hair. A moment later he pushed the fabric of her panties to the side, and when his tongue touched her flesh she couldn't stop herself from tightening her grip on him. Nor could she stop her hips from coming up off the bed, seeking more.

And he gave more.

A lot more.

He kept going for the next few minutes, with skill she'd never in her life experienced before now. The orgasm that overcame her was all-consuming. Her legs shook. Her body arched. And the room was filled with her panting his name.

Panting.

He brought her down slowly, his mouth not pausing from its ministrations. Her hands loosened from their death grip in his hair and fell to the bed. She opened her eyes and it took her a second to focus.

Logan kissed the inside of her thigh before he moved up her body. He placed open mouth kisses along her belly.

"You smell good everywhere. *Everywhere.*" His lips brushed her skin, the warm touch of his breath washing over her as he pushed her sweater up past her breasts. He ran his tongue underneath the swells, pulling at the thin fabric with his teeth.

"I need you naked," he murmured right before his mouth opened up on a fabric-covered nipple.

Abby had no idea where the strength, or energy for that matter, came from. Hello, he'd just *destroyed* her with his mouth. But she pulled her legs up again, wrapping them around his waist and rolling.

Now she was the one looking down at him, and she couldn't help grinning at the man beneath her.

What *was* she going to do with him?

* * *

The move had caught Logan off guard and that was the only reason he was currently on his back. There'd been no doubt in his mind that he could've stopped Abby from rolling him over. He guessed he had about eighty pounds on her, so it wouldn't have been all that hard.

But why would he have stopped her? A beautiful woman had all but mounted him, and he'd be lying if he didn't have images of her riding him long and hard. But he was going to let her call the shots, and as she looked down at his body, he knew she had plans.

She reached for her sweater first—it was still bunched above her breasts—and pulled it up and over her head.

"I think it's my turn now." She placed her palms flat on his abs, adjusting herself on his lap and lightly grinding against his already very hard dick.

He swallowed, trying to restrain himself. He wanted to reach up and grab her hips, wanted to guide her into moving against him harder. But as much as he wanted to do that, he wanted to see what she was going to do more.

"I think that sounds perfect."

She smiled as she ran her hands up his body. Her hair fell forward as she moved, the strands stretching down and tickling his skin. She hovered over him now, those blue eyes of hers focused on his.

"Good," she said right before she lowered her mouth to his.

Words couldn't express how much he loved the taste of her mouth. Warm and sweet and just the right amount of spice. And as she explored his mouth with hers, she obliterated his brain when she started moving her hips, grinding against him.

At least he'd thought she'd obliterated his brain. Because as she started to move her mouth down his torso, he realized he'd been wrong. Oh, so very wrong.

She started kissing down the trail of hair leading from his belly button and all the way past the waistband of his jeans. And then she was unfastening the button, pulling down the zipper, and shoving his pants down his thighs. She only got them far enough down his legs for his erection to spring free.

It took everything in him not to buck off the bed when her tongue darted out and wrapped around the tip of his cock.

"Holy hell, Abby!" he managed to get out. But the next string of words out of his mouth weren't all that coherent, because her mouth covered the head while her hand worked the base.

This time his hands did come up, his fingers spearing in her hair, because he had to touch her. Had to feel her moving over him.

And that was how he stayed for the next few minutes, enjoying every single fucking second until he couldn't take it anymore.

"I..." He had to swallow hard, trying to find words. "I'm going to come."

The warm wetness of her mouth disappeared and she looked up at him, grinning wide. "What are you waiting for?" she asked before her mouth returned to its earlier mission.

He let himself go over to it. *All* of it. Savoring the feel of her mouth on him. Savoring her touch.

It was then that her hand dropped for just a second, lightly squeezing his balls.

He lost it, unable to stop himself from arching off the bed. Abby's mouth stayed on him till the end, sucking him dry.

And this time it was Logan sinking into the mattress trying to remember how to breathe.

* * *

Abby had never pictured Logan James as a snuggler, but here she was, wrapped in his arms and pressed up against his chest. His hand lazily trailed up and down her spine. She was good and thoroughly exhausted, but so content it was ridiculous.

Logan had needed a little bit of time to recuperate, but once he had, he didn't hesitate to pin her down onto the mattress and make her lose her mind again.

And again.

And again.

She ran her hand up his chest as she tipped her head back to look at him. He moved, too, his mouth coming down on hers. He rolled her onto her back, giving her a slow kiss that curled her toes and threatened to set the sheets on fire.

Then he pulled away just far enough to focus those gold-green eyes of his on her. "You going to pull away from me again tomorrow morning?" he asked as he reached up and brushed a piece of her hair behind her ear.

"No." She shook her head. "But how is this going to work?"

He shifted, rolling to his side and propping his head up on his arm. He ran his other hand down her neck, across her collarbone, and to her chest. He palmed one of her breasts as he traced her nipple with the pad of his thumb.

She was unable to stop the shiver of pleasure that ran through her...something that had happened for about the hundredth time that night.

"We just make it work."

"Sneaking around?"

"I prefer to think of it as keeping things private," he said as he dipped his head and kissed her collarbone.

"And what about the fact that you're a client who despises what I do with every fiber of your being?"

He brought his gaze back up to her and grinned. "We'll figure it out."

"So we go into this with no plan?"

"We do have a plan. We keep your job and reputation intact, and my private life stays out of the news. Really this is the optimum situation. For once we have a common goal."

"I don't think it's going to be all that simple."

"Simple is entirely overrated." His hand skimmed down her body. He paused at her belly for just a second before he continued south. When he got to her knees he pulled her legs apart and rolled, settling between her thighs. "I'll take complicated any day."

He lowered his mouth to hers, and all thoughts of anything besides his body moving over hers magically vacated her brain.

Chapter 5

Stampede Indeed

The sharp *clip clip clip* of Abby's red high heels echoed off the concrete walls around her. The hallway leading to the Jacksonville Stampede locker room was more like a tunnel than anything else, and it amplified any and all noise. And, oh boy, was there some noise when all twenty-nine testosterone-filled men were coming down the passageway.

How appropriate that the team's mascot was a raging bunch of wild animals.

It had been a month since Abby and Logan had returned from Mirabelle. A month since they'd embarked on their relationship, and they'd been pretty good at keeping it a secret.

As Logan had said, they'd figured it out.

They'd spent over half of those nights together, either at his house, her condo, or in various hotel rooms when they were on the road. She always had her own room, so he stayed in hers. Whenever she'd get her room keys, she'd just pass one off to him and he'd show up shortly after…and stay through the night.

Working and sleeping with Logan hadn't been an issue…yet.

Abby's focus had been almost exclusively devoted on the charity dinner auction for St. Ignatius. The hospital was in the process of raising funds to rebuild their cancer wing, and they'd enlisted the help of the Stampede.

Much like going to visit Dale, the auction wasn't something that Logan had fought her on when it came to his participation. His brother, Liam James, was an up and coming country musician, and Logan had snagged some backstage VIP tickets for the tour that Liam was opening for.

The headlining band was Isaac Hunter, a country duo that was currently tearing up the charts. It also didn't hurt that both men were beyond handsome and looked so good in a pair of jeans and boots that it should be illegal.

Not only would the winners get to go to the concert the night the tour stopped through Jacksonville, but they'd also get to eat dinner with Logan, Liam, Isaac, and Hunter. It was guaranteed to be a lethal combination of attractive men around that table. She had no doubts that the women at the auction would be bidding on the four-ticket evening like crazy.

Abby had been more than surprised with the package that Logan had offered up. Not only did it involve him in the public eye, but it involved him being social. She knew he was more than capable of doing it, he just didn't like to.

But she wasn't getting used to his cooperation. She had no doubts on his earlier promise of being just as difficult as he'd always been when it came to things that he didn't agree with. It didn't mean she wasn't going to ride this wave for as long as possible, though.

But today Logan wasn't her mission. Kent Proctor was the intended target, the only player who hadn't put something up for the auction. If there was a bigger problem on the Stampede, she didn't know. He'd been drafted to the NHL when he was eighteen, and the five years he'd been in the league hadn't improved his problem-child behavior.

He was excellent on the ice. Off of it? Not so much.

He was arrogant, immature, and beyond difficult to work with. He made Logan look like a freaking angel.

Abby took a deep breath and straightened her shoulders before she pushed through the doors and walked into the locker room. A handful of players were standing in front of their lockers in varying stages of undress.

This wasn't the optimum place to talk to anyone, but desperate times called for desperate measures and this was sometimes the only place she could corner a few of the players, especially the problem children.

After Abby got the job, she quickly had to get used to being around half-naked—or sometimes entirely naked—men. Being in a locker room was not always a pleasant experience. It was generally smelly and hot, and oh-so-very crowded. It was a bit of an obstacle course navigating through the tape, sweaty jerseys, and pads that littered the floor. Not to mention the massive human bodies that were either elated after their win, or pissed after their loss.

The guys were used to the varying forms of staff and reporters being in there. They weren't exactly going to swing their junk, genitals or otherwise, at her. They had to work with her on a daily basis, not to mention Coach Anthony Bale wouldn't put up with that for a second.

Besides, the only body that had ever really distracted her had been Logan's…and that was both before and after things had started up. Being able to see him up close and personal when they were in private didn't make it any easier when she was in the locker room with so many other eyes around. If anything, it was harder now.

When the two of them were alone together, they always had their hands on each other. When they were in public, she constantly had to keep herself in check. It was different, this feeling of always wanting to touch him. Of always wanting him to touch her. She'd never experienced it before. Not with any other guy.

Just the thought of his lips brushing across the back of her neck had the ability to make her shiver. And as her eyes landed on him, she did just that. The shiver was such a contrast to the fact that he simultaneously got her all hot and bothered.

Yup, she was so screwed.

He made it impossible to stay calm, cool, and collected when he was only wearing a pair of jeans. His light brown hair was sticking up from where he'd carelessly dried it with his towel, and his muscles rippled with every movement as he dug around in his bag.

One would think after the time they'd spent together she'd be a little bit more in control of herself.

They would be wrong. He made her palms sweaty.

Focus, woman!

He was talking to his teammate Jace Kilpatrick, who just so happened to be Logan's best friend. Abby liked Jace. He was a sweet, good-natured guy and more than a bit of a playboy, not all that surprising with his shaggy dark blond hair, aquamarine eyes, and mischievous grin.

He was constantly on the front covers of tabloids with the newest leggy model or actress. His last girlfriend was a very famous singer, Veronica Trumbower. Before their breakup, which she hadn't taken very well, there'd been an incident where the paparazzi had caught them in a less than delicate position in a private club. The thing was, no one should've known that they were there. The security on the place was ridiculous, so it appeared that someone had been tipped off.

Veronica wrote a song about the whole relationship, which had very little good and a ton of bad and ugly. It had stayed at number one for months.

That had been delightful to deal with.

Logan pulled a T-shirt out of his bag and as he straightened, his head came up and those green-gold eyes of his landed on her. His mouth quirked to the side as he did a quick scan of her body, landing on her heels.

They were the same red ones she'd worn the first night they had sex.

When he returned his gaze to hers, there was a heat in his eyes that made way more than her palms sweaty. She gave him a warning look, but it just made that quirk on his mouth turn into a grin.

"I haven't seen you down here in a while, Red." He started to pull his shirt up his arms. "You been busy?" he asked, his head disappearing into his shirt for just a second before it popped up through the neck hole and he adjusted the hem around his waist.

She immediately missed the sight of his muscles. But at least her brain started functioning again.

"Yes." She nodded. "Trying to get the final details worked out for the St. Ignatius dinner." Something that he knew as pretty much all of her spare time was spent with him. She'd had to work on it more than a few of the nights they'd been together.

"I hear it's going to be a fancy event. Got to get my suit cleaned if I'm going to try and impress." Jace waggled his eyebrows as he grinned at her.

He hadn't given her any grief for the evening, either. His package up for bid was a brand-new surfboard and five surfing lessons with Jace himself. Not only was he a damn good hockey player, but he was a licensed surf instructor as well.

Who knew?

He'd grown up in LA, spending his time out on the ice rinks and the ocean in equal part. Needless to say he had superb balancing skills.

"You're going to need a lot more than a suit to help you there, buddy." Logan shook his head.

"Says the man with limited social skills."

Logan's eyes narrowed as he shook his head at Jace. "I have more skills than you could dream of, pal."

"I'll leave you two to work this little debate out on your own." Abby smiled as she gestured between the two men. "Let me know who wins."

"Will do," Jace said.

But before Abby moved off, her gaze met Logan's one last time, catching the longing that gleamed in his eyes. She forced herself to look away and move across the room, where Kent Proctor was talking to none other than Rodger Dingle.

Well, apparently this battle was going to be hard fought.

Abby was well used to being underestimated. It was something she'd constantly had to deal with before this job, and it hadn't been any easier when walking into a testosterone-ridden environment.

Dingle also worked in the Stampede PR department, and he hadn't been a fan of Abby since the moment she'd been hired, nor had he been quiet about his opinions, either. He hadn't dealt well with the facts that she was seven years his junior, that he had been working with the Stampede for five years now, and that they pretty much had the exact same position. Not to mention the added bonus that she was a woman.

He constantly tried to undermine her no matter the audience. He would withhold information from her, giving her press releases at the last minute. Or somehow forgetting to mention a connection or important detail and making himself look like the hero when he "had to step up" to fix the situation. She'd put in all the effort and he would try to take the credit with one little detail.

Too bad it was going to take a lot more than that to throw her off. She'd dealt with bigger jerks than him. He couldn't have forgotten that she'd worked in politics for *years*.

Really he could be considered attractive with his short black hair and strong jaw, but when he opened his mouth and actually spoke, any and all possibilities of attractiveness went out the window.

Plus his last name was Dingle.

"D.C.," he said as he looked her up and down with that sneer of his. She tried not to flinch at the nickname. She knew what it meant. Had heard him mutter it under his breath many times. He played the whole thing off as her coming from Washington before she'd moved down here.

Too bad she knew it meant Damn Cunt.

"Rodger. Kent." She smiled at both men politely.

"What brings you to the locker rooms? You know this isn't any place for a *lady*."

She again forced herself to ignore the fact that Dingle believed she wasn't all that welcome in the locker room. *It's a man's world*, he'd said on multiple occasions. *What the hell does she know about this sport?*

She actually knew a lot of things about the sport. She'd grown up watching it with her grandfather, had gone to more Philadelphia Flyers games than she could count.

"I needed to speak with Mr. Proctor here. I was wondering if you had a chance to decide what you wanted to do for the charity dinner. We need to get everything turned in by the end of the week so the hospital knows what to expect."

"Waiting until the last minute I see?" Dingle asked, clicking his tongue as he shook his head.

"What charity dinner?" Proctor asked, his eyebrows bunching together.

"And not informing everyone who is supposed to be involved? Sounds like you're on the ball."

Deep breaths. Deep. Breaths.

"The St. Ignatius dinner at the end of the month. We're doing an auction to raise money for the new cancer wing," Abby explained patiently.

"We are? I don't remember this."

It took everything in Abby to keep her practiced smile plastered across her face. Not only had she had many, *many*, conversations with the team about this, but she'd also sent out multiple reminders. Not to mention the fact that she'd had her assistant Brooke talk to the players on numerous occasions. Proctor's response of "I'll deal with it later" was the only thing that Brooke could report back.

"You should," came a voice from behind Abby.

She turned to the side as Captain Andre Fabian strolled toward her. He was a huge man. A good two hundred and fifteen pounds of what was probably solid muscle and standing tall at six-foot-five. He had thick dark brown hair, severe eyebrows that were currently turned down, and a frown that would make lesser men cower.

He was from Winnipeg, his time in the south not changing his accent at all. He wasn't one of those apologetic Canadians, either. She'd never heard an unearned *I'm sorry* coming out of his mouth. That wasn't to say he wasn't a good guy; he just didn't mess around.

A force to be reckoned with, on and off the ice.

The only time she'd seen that face of his entirely intimidation free was when he was holding his two-year-old son in his arms.

Count on a child to bring a man to his knees.

"Proctor, I know that you have listening issues when it doesn't involve a hot brunette praising your prowess, but this dinner isn't something new."

"It doesn't have to be a hot brunette." Proctor shrugged. "A redhead would do just fine."

A fire that Abby had never seen flashed in Andre's eyes, but she only caught a glimpse of it. She was distracted by Logan who was making his way across the locker room.

"You better watch yourself," Andre said, taking a step into Kent's space. "And you better start paying attention, because you acting like a dick will reflect badly on the entire team."

"Fine. Fine." Proctor held up his hands. "Have whatever minion working under you send me the forms."

Andre nodded before he moved off to his locker at the end of the row.

"My assistant Brooke can send them again."

"Brooke…" Proctor trailed off. "Blonde? Long legs? Has a thing for pink lipstick?"

"Yes," Abby said slowly, not appreciating the look in Proctor's eyes one bit.

"Looking forward to it."

Abby took a step back from the group, turning just in time to see Logan pass by her, a frown on his face as he headed for the showers and bathrooms behind them. She'd walked about three steps when she heard Proctor speak again, in a voice that carried easily through the room.

"You know, dealing with her would be a lot more pleasant if she was on her knees at some point during the encounter."

Abby didn't even have time to turn around before the thud hit her ears. When her eyes landed on the scene behind her, she froze. Logan had Proctor pinned up against the wall, his arm braced against Proctor's chest and his face inches away from Proctor's.

* * *

It had been a long time since Logan had been so angry that he was actually shaking with rage. A long time since he'd been so blinded by it that it had taken over his body and forced him into action.

He'd never liked Proctor, had always thought that the guy was a hot-headed, egotistical little prick. Hearing him talk about any woman like that would've pissed Logan off. But hearing him talk about Abby? No fucking way.

"Apologize." The low growl that rumbled out of his chest sounded foreign to his own ears.

"Get off me." Proctor pushed at Logan's arm unsuccessfully.

"After you apologize. It is *never* okay to say something like that. Not to any woman. Not *ever*. Do you understand me?"

"James, I don't give a flying fuck what you think. Get your hands off me."

Logan shifted, grabbing the front of Kent's shirt and pulling him off the wall before shoving him back into it. "You're a disgusting piece of shit. You know that?"

"Logan, come on. Ease up." Hands were on Logan's shoulder. Hands pulling him away from the wall and forcing him to let go. "He isn't worth it."

"What the hell is going on in here?" A booming voice filled the room. Logan looked over as Coach Anthony Bale and two other guys in suits walked out of the office in the back. Bale's face had reached that shade of red that meant danger…either that or Logan was just seeing the color everywhere.

His hands were shaking and he had to ball them up into fists. Probably not the best idea, though, as it made him one step closer to punching Proctor in the face.

It was then Logan realized it was Jace who had pulled him off Proctor. His friend hadn't let go, either, still gripping Logan's shoulders as they both continued to move backward. Andre was moving, too, now standing in the space that had been created between Logan and the biggest asshole in the room.

It didn't take Coach Bale very long to figure out what had been going on. His gaze ran through the space before he looked between Logan and Proctor. "Fight in my locker room again and none of you are going to like what happens after. Understood?"

"Yes, sir." Logan nodded.

"Won't happen again," Proctor said.

Bale didn't say anything else as he turned around and headed back to his office, the two suited men following him. Logan turned around to find Abby standing behind him, the shock in her face evident.

He wanted so much to reach out and touch her. Wanted to pull her into his body and make it clear to every guy in this room that she wasn't a woman to be insulted, wasn't a woman to be messed with in any way, shape, or form. That she was his and he wouldn't hesitate to defend her, no matter the circumstances.

It didn't matter what Bale had said. If Proctor ever insulted Abby again he would be getting a fist in the face sooner than later, and it would be Logan doing it.

* * *

"You've *got* to be kidding me."

It was taking everything in Logan to not start screaming. But as they were in Abby's condo and the walls weren't all that thick, he somehow managed.

It had been two days since the locker room incident. ESPN had gotten ahold of the story within a few hours, and they were having a fucking field day with it.

Trouble in Parad-Ice?

Why is James giving Proctor the cold shoulder?

Are the Stampede Melting Under the Pressure?

It was unfortunate that the two suits in Bale's office were part of the press. But as they hadn't been in the locker room during the actual altercation, they shouldn't have known the reason behind it. Multiple reports had included the lovely little tidbit about the fact that the fight had been over a woman. And it hadn't taken very long for them to figure out that it was Abby.

That had sparked the old debate about women being in locker rooms.

Logan had been avoiding reporters for the last couple of days, leaving the statements in the hands of the Stampede PR department. Though as Abby had been involved, this problem had been passed off to that smarmy prick that Logan avoided at all costs. His name was Dillweed, or Dipshit, or Dickhead, or something.

And now Abby was telling Logan that the two of them had

to cool things down for a little bit. With both of them on the radar, they couldn't take any chances.

It pissed him off to a level that he couldn't really begin to process.

"I was defending you." He'd come over here thinking they were going to get to spend the evening together. Order a pizza, drink some wine, have some crazy hot monkey sex...

But no. The pizza was getting cold, the wine warm, and his frustration was growing.

"I know, Logan." Abby closed her eyes as she rested her palm against her forehead.

"So that asshole insults you and I get punished?"

"You think that I want any of this?" Her hand dropped as she looked at him. "The whole situation has caused a huge headache with the press. It's taking everyone—"

"I don't care about the stupid press!"

"You should! You getting into a fight with a teammate in the locker room isn't something small. It has to be dealt with delicately so that it doesn't become worse."

"And if we could just tell the fucking truth, then it wouldn't be like this. If people knew what Proctor had said to you, the exact vile words that came out of his mouth, there would be no debating what was going on."

"It doesn't work that way. It's the entire team's image that we have to worry about."

"Why?" he asked as he ran his hands through his hair, making it stand on end.

Abby took a deep breath and shook her head as she let it out slowly. "You guys are a month away from the playoffs and right now you're the top team. So this is the way it has to be, Logan. "

"It's bullshit."

"I know that. I don't want this, either." She made a step toward him, reaching out. "I don't—" But she stopped midsentence when Logan took a step away from her touch.

The hurt in her eyes managed to somehow make him angrier. Deep down—way, *way* deep down—he knew she was just doing her job. But it didn't change the fact that he felt she was choosing sides. And it wasn't his.

He was being punished for defending her, *protecting* her, and it pissed him off.

"We have to cool things down. Remember?"

He turned and grabbed his leather jacket from where he'd tossed it on the back of the sofa and headed for the door.

Chapter 6

The Joys of Family Dinners

Logan wasn't a fan of the nights that he didn't get to spend with Abby. He definitely preferred going to bed curled around her warm body as opposed to going to bed alone. He also thoroughly enjoyed waking up next to her. And it wasn't just an *anybody*-being-in-his-bed kind of thing. It was *her* being in his bed.

He wasn't sure when it had happened. When it had become about her laugh in his ear, her warm breath washing across his skin, and that smile of hers turning up against his throat a second before she'd kiss him.

He missed her, missed her way more than he should after only a handful of weeks together.

But he did.

They'd had very little interaction because the team had been traveling with away games and Abby hadn't been on the road with them. She was working hard on the dinner that was two days away. It had been taking up most of her focus before, so he was sure she was even more preoccupied now. He had no doubt she was stressed, but as they weren't exactly talking, he didn't know.

It had been two weeks since Logan's fight with Proctor, and every reporter covering the pre-game, actual game, or post-game still liked to mention it.

The media's favorite time to bring it up and start dissecting it like a lab experiment? When Logan and Proctor were on the ice at the same time.

Logan was doing his best not to give the press anything else to work with...which was difficult. He blamed Proctor for the fact that he was *still* missing evenings with Abby. He wasn't pleased about it in the slightest.

At least he had a pretty decent distraction tonight, and it came in the form of his little sister Adele. She was making their grandmother's paella, the only person besides their mother who could do it justice.

Logan had invited Jace over as well. His friend had a thing about home-cooked meals, probably because they'd been few and far between growing up in the Kilpatrick household. His mother died when he was eight, and his father was a renowned heart surgeon who was hardly ever at home.

Jace wasn't exactly close with his father. In fact, they had very little to do with each other. Dr. Ferguson Kilpatrick didn't approve of his son's career. He wasn't impressed at all, actually.

Jace was drafted to the Stampede a year after Logan was traded. They worked well together as team players and had become friends off the ice, as well. Logan wasn't one to get close to anyone over the last couple of years, but Jace had somehow worked his way in. He'd spent the last four Christmases with Logan and his family.

A close family was something else that Jace missed, and distance or not, Logan's family was incredibly close-knit.

Logan's parents had sold their house years ago and now

traveled all across North America. They were currently making their way up the Pacific Coast. Their destination? Alaska.

His brother Liam was a lot like his parents these days. The guy was constantly on the road jumping from tour to tour. Whenever he needed a home base for a few weeks, he stayed at the cabin in Nashville.

Adele and Logan were the only two who actually had homes, and they lived about fifteen minutes from each other. She had even picked out Logan's house.

It was a three-story gothic revival home, with a front and back porch, a six-car garage filled with his various motored toys, a pool, and a dock that moored his sailboat. The Intracoastal Waterway was only a couple hundred yards from his back door.

Adele had taken one loop around the house with its original hardwood floors and informed him he had to buy it. He told her only if she decorated. He didn't have to twist her arm very much before she agreed. But as she had a fantastic attention to detail and her design aesthetic went well beyond clothing, it made perfect sense.

Adele was the head costume designer on the hit show *Ponce*. It took place in St. Augustine at the Ponce de Leon Hotel during the early nineteen hundreds. It was the Florida version of *Downton Abbey*.

She had the ability to capture any era perfectly, and her own style fluctuated anywhere in the last century. Tonight she was rocking the fifties, her dark brown hair curled and pinned up. It was held back with a yellow and white polka-dotted bandanna. She somehow made the whole look work with her pierced nose and the streaks of bright red in her hair.

"So are you going to tell me about this whole Proctor thing?" she asked about a second after they sat down at the dinner table.

Logan looked at his sister as he took a bite of his meal, chewing slowly and trying to formulate his words. She might be seven years younger than him—and the baby of the family—but she was just as much of a protector for him and their middle brother Liam as they were for her.

Though as Logan saw her on a regular basis, he got the brunt of it.

Adele's golden brown eyes were just as sharp as their mother's, and she missed very little. She could be intimidating as hell. She got it from their mother's Spanish side of the family. Though to be fair, their father's Irish side had a good amount of those qualities, as well.

"What about it?" Logan asked before he reached for his beer.

"Seriously?" Adele frowned. "For someone who doesn't like to make a spectacle of himself, you pushing a player against the wall in front of reporters—whether the guy is a good-for-nothing prick or not—is a step in the wrong direction. So why did you snap over what he said to this Abby woman?"

"Because he's dating that Abby woman," Jace said from his side of the table.

Logan choked on his beer. "What?" he asked when he could breathe again. Apparently he and Abby hadn't been as stealthy in their sneaking around as they'd thought.

Adele's attention swiveled to Jace. She pointed her fork at him as her eyes narrowed. "Start talking."

"Logan and one Ms. Abby Fields, more commonly referred to as Red by him and him alone, have been seeing each other for over a month now." Jace's grin was so huge that Logan was tempted to reach across the table and punch the smug little shit in the face.

"How the hell did you know?"

"It wasn't exactly detective work. You've been eyeing her since she showed up. And ever since you went on that little trip with her on Valentine's Day, you haven't been coming back to your room when we're on the road. Or you weren't until about two weeks ago when the whole incident happened."

"Is that so?" Adele asked. "Huh, well isn't this interesting?"

"You notice that he smiles more? Or did. Something else that changed about two weeks ago. Del, your brother has been particularly pissy of late, but my guess is that's because he hasn't been able to spend any time with a certain redhead."

"You're an asshole." Logan shook his head at Jace.

"No, you're the asshole," Adele said now, pointing her fork at Logan. "Two questions—"

"Just two?" he asked, raising his eyebrows at her.

Her eyes somehow narrowed even more. "To start with. Number one is: why haven't you introduced me to your girlfriend yet?"

"She isn't my girlfriend," Logan said as he grabbed his beer from the table and leaned back in his seat.

"Then what is she?" Adele's eyebrows furrowed. "You better not say fuck buddy."

This time it was Jace choking on his beer. "I'm so glad I don't have siblings to grill me about my sex life."

"They'd never get to the bottom of *your* sex life, Jace." The look that Adele shot him was scorching.

Logan felt bad for his friend for about a second. But then Adele returned her focus on him and he tried not to squirm in his chair. "Start talking, big brother," she demanded.

Why did he surround himself with such intense women?

Though, being in a relationship with a woman like Abby was a new thing. She wasn't like any woman he'd gone for before.

"So if she's not your girlfriend, then what is she?" Adele asked.

"A girl who I'm seeing."

"With the possibility of something serious?"

"I don't know."

This was true...he didn't know what this was with Abby, hadn't known from the moment it had started. All he did know was that he wanted her, had from the first time he'd seen her. That fact hadn't changed.

"But you like her?"

More than he was prepared to admit. In any other relationship, the complications that he was currently dealing with would have had him moving on in an instant. He wasn't moving on from her. And that was a detail he was choosing not to analyze all that much.

"Yes." He nodded.

"Talking to you is like pulling teeth." Adele was so exasperated with him that he was surprised she hadn't thrown her fork at him yet. "Why didn't I know about this?"

"Because we aren't telling people."

"I'm not *people*, Logan."

It was then that he realized she was hurt, hurt about his keeping her in the dark. But how was a person supposed to shed light on a situation that they themselves didn't even understand?

"I'm sorry, Adele."

"I don't know how I feel about you being in a secret relationship, either. Is that her deal or yours? Because any woman in her right mind wouldn't want to keep you a secret."

Logan couldn't stop the small smile that twitched at his lips. "Thanks, but the secretiveness is necessary. She's a publicist for the team. Apparently there's a no fraternization clause in her contract."

"Seriously?" Jace asked.

"Yeah, so you better keep your mouth shut."

"Dude, I've pretty much known since it started and didn't say a word."

"Until now." Logan frowned.

"And maybe that's a good thing," Adele said pointedly. "This whole thing proves that you aren't as slick as you think you are, sneaking around."

"Oh, I think it proves a lot more than that," Jace said.

"And what's that?" Logan asked.

"What Proctor did was a dick move, there are no doubts about that. But your reaction was…intense. Sure, you might've gotten in his face if he'd insulted any woman, but I thought you were about to shove his head through the wall. And maybe it's because I know you more than most, but the look on your face was not one of a man who 'doesn't know what it is' when it comes to the woman he's currently seeing." Jace's statement came complete with air quotes and a pitying shake of the head.

"How about the two of you not worry about it? Look, it's the perfect situation. She can't be in a public relationship with me and I hate having my private life in the public eye. It's working."

Or at least it had been.

"Hmmm," Adele hummed as she studied her brother. "I'm going to need more evidence."

"Well, good luck collecting it," he said, tipping his beer bottle to her before he took a sip. He wasn't able to spend any time with Abby lately, so he didn't know how Adele was going to get any information on the situation. "So what was the second question?"

"Jace said you went somewhere with her?"

"Yeah." He nodded slowly, putting his bottle back on the table. "A friend of Abby's is a teacher over in Mirabelle, Florida. One of her students has cancer. He's seventeen years old and just had a tumor removed from his brain. Should make a full recovery, but he was having some difficulty with the chemo. "

Some of the harshness left Adele's face as she looked at her brother. "How was that?"

"I've done easier things." Logan looked down to his dinner to scoop up another bite and he caught a glimpse of Jace's now somber face.

Jace was the only one on the team who knew about Madison. On the fifth anniversary of her death, Logan had been at the bar in whatever hotel the Stampede was staying. He didn't even remember; that time of year he tended to function on autopilot.

Jace had joined him when he was a couple of drinks in, and somewhere along the way the story had slipped out.

It wasn't that Logan had kept his daughter a secret because he was ashamed of her. Not in any way, shape, or form was that the case. From the second she was born he'd been hell bent on protecting her. She'd already had a crap mother. Cassidy had been in and out of Madison's life, showing up whenever she felt like it and leaving just as quickly. So he'd been bound and determined to do everything in his power to shelter his daughter from anything else.

Turns out, there were some things that were impossible to shelter her from.

As Madison had Cassidy's last name—something that Cassidy had done to spite him—no one had made the connection that her father was the now famous hockey player Logan James. Besides, that was before Logan had been anything really notable on the ice.

After college, Logan spent two years in the minor leagues where pretty much no one was paying attention to him. Life had been a lot simpler then, and he'd been happy.

He forgot what that was like.

It was a year after Madison's death when he was drafted to the majors. He played for the Detroit Redwings for two years, the first of which he spent more time on the bench than anyone else on the team. Then he'd been off to Florida where it was another couple of years before his career had taken off and his name started to show up on a regular basis in the wide world of sports news.

A close group of friends, both from college and when he was in the minors, had obviously known about Madison. But as they were close, they obviously respected his privacy and his wishes. So she wasn't a story that the press knew to look for. And he hoped it stayed that way.

So yeah, it wasn't about keeping his daughter a secret, it was more that her memory was sacred. Something he kept close at all times. She wasn't a story to be exploited, or talked about. She was to be cherished, and that was something strangers couldn't do.

No, only those who knew her could do it. Those who loved her.

The table around Logan was quiet for entirely too long, and the silence made him twitchy. He cleared his throat before he looked up, his eyes landing on his sister first. He knew she was tempted to reach over and touch his hand, but he was glad she refrained.

Adele knew that being around a kid with cancer was bound to remind Logan of Madison, and whenever it came to things with his daughter he was too raw. That was something he didn't want to deal with at the moment. And after spending his evenings over the last two weeks alone, he'd been particularly vulnerable.

Logan had long since been used to nights where he'd fall

asleep on his sofa with the TV running and an empty glass of scotch balanced on his knee. But things were better when he'd been seeing Abby on a regular basis, when he'd spent evenings with her feet in his lap while they sat outside on his back porch. When they ordered room service in the hotel rooms and ate breakfast wrapped in bathrobes after they showered together, when he got to feel her against him...she made everything *better.*

That bottomless sadness that he was always fighting hadn't reared its ugly head. No, it had been kept at bay, pushed to a place where there wasn't that constant dull ache. He'd also been without those days where it was a blinding stabbing pain.

Better. Abby just made things *better.* And this whole not getting to see her wasn't working for him.

Not in the slightest.

Chapter 7

An Evening of Surprises

Abby had been running around like a crazy person for the last hour working on the final touches for the St. Ignatius charity dinner. When she finally walked into the ballroom of the Brogan-Meyers Hotel, it was packed with men in suits and women in designer gowns.

"Champagne?" a waiter asked, coming up next to her.

"Thank you." She smiled, nodding at him as she grabbed a glass from the tray.

She took a sip, letting the cold bubbles trickle down her throat. She closed her eyes in pleasure and took just a moment to enjoy what she knew was a very expensive bottle.

But when she opened her eyes, her moment of pleasure was gone.

Logan was standing on the other side of the room with a stunning brunette. The woman was wearing a gorgeous cream flapper dress, the delicate fringe hitting her just above the knees of her long legs. Two strands of pearls hung from her neck, satin gloves up to her elbows, and her hair pulled back with a rather elaborate headpiece.

It could have looked costumey, but she pulled it off in spades.

One of Logan's arms was wrapped around her waist and he was laughing as she leaned against him and whispered something in his ear. Then she moved her mouth and placed a soft kiss on his cheek.

The jealousy that bubbled in Abby's belly had nothing, *nothing*, to do with the champagne.

He came with a date? He came with a *fucking* date?

Okay, yes they'd had an argument, they'd been cooling things down over the last couple of weeks, but she didn't think that they'd broken up.

Broken up?

Was it even at that point? They'd never talked about being exclusive or discussed anything about their "relationship." The only thing they'd discussed was exploring wherever "things" would go.

Apparently he was done exploring. He'd just forgotten to tell her.

She wasn't even remotely prepared for the sinking disappointment that hit her, and that combined with the jealousy that was coursing through her was potent.

But she refused to be hurt by him. *Refused.*

She tipped the glass back and took a mouthful of champagne before she turned away. But she wasn't going to be given even a minute to collect herself. Rodger Dingle was making his way over to her, that smarmy smile of his that she despised so much leading the way.

"D.C., I see you're pulling out *all* the stops tonight." His eyes moved up and down her body, taking in her red dress.

It was formfitting, clinging to all of her curves and stopping just short of her knees. The top was a halter and showed just a hint of cleavage. It was sexy no doubt, but in no way immodest. Though she was now immediately regretting her decision to wear it, and not because of the way Dingle was looking at her.

No, she regretted it because she'd specifically chosen it for Logan. He liked her in red, and she thought it would be a nice first step in attempting to smooth things over with him.

Well, hadn't she been spectacularly wrong?

"I always pull out all the stops. I guess you aren't familiar with what that looks like."

His eyes narrowed on her and he took a step forward, dipping his head down close to her ear. "I think that your reign as the golden child is going to run out very soon," he whispered before he moved off.

Well, tonight was already off to a fantastic start. But she refused to let any of these jerks get to her. *Refused*. She'd worked too damn hard for this night, had started working on it almost immediately after she'd been hired. This event was for an amazing cause, something much bigger than an ended fling or a bitter co-worker.

She took a deep breath before she finished off the last of her champagne, determined to get her head back in it…and her heart?

Well, who the hell cared about that?

* * *

Logan had noticed Abby the second she'd walked into the room, and he was doing everything in his power to not openly stare at her. The dress she was wearing looked like it had been painted on, and his fingers itched to peel her out of it.

Her auburn hair was curled and hanging down around her

shoulders, and she was wearing a pair of black heels that he would be dreaming about for the rest of his life.

"So that's her?" Adele asked as they sat down at the dinner table.

He had been beyond surprised to find Adele here when he walked into the ballroom tonight. He wasn't at all prepared for her presence. Apparently the cast and crew of *Ponce* had all been invited to the event, something Adele had conveniently left out of every conversation over the last few weeks.

She hadn't wanted Logan to know she was coming, the element of surprise and all. He was pretty sure it was a reconnaissance mission now more than anything else. He knew his sister, and she was eager to figure out what was going on with him and Abby.

Well, she wasn't the only one.

"Yeah." He nodded, pulling his gaze from Abby.

"She's beautiful."

"She's a lot of things, and her beauty isn't even half of it."

Adele's eyes went wide and her mouth split into a grin. "Well, that's high praise from you."

"It's the truth." His eyes moved back in the direction he'd seen her last, landing on her in an instant.

God he missed her. They were going to get this whole thing resolved tonight. He wasn't going to let this problem with Proctor keep him from what he wanted for another fucking night.

Though, that wasn't something he could take care of at the moment. She was talking to Willis Fisher, the owner of the team, and two other men in tuxes. Logan liked Fisher all right, or at least he thought he did. Because a second later he was restraining himself from jumping out of his seat and pulling Abby away from the group of men.

Abby's assistant Brooke came up to the group and as Abby excused herself to step aside, the other men all took the opportunity to check both women out as they walked out of the ballroom.

It was the first time the word *mine* had ever sounded in Logan's head loud and clear when it came to a woman.

There was a certainty to it that he knew all too well. It was the gut feeling he got whenever he was on the ice. When instinct ruled all and everything else went by the wayside.

He'd had it when it came to Madison and her diagnosis. So many doctors hadn't been able to figure out what was wrong with her. But he'd known that his daughter was sick and he hadn't rested until they'd figured it out.

He'd never run from his instincts before. Never went in the opposite direction when his gut was screaming at him to take action.

And he wasn't going to now, either.

That was what had him standing up. *That* was what had him walking out the doors and looking for Abby.

* * *

The chair on the board of directors for St. Ignatius had wanted a quick word with Abby before dinner started. Over the last few months, Gemma Faro had been nothing but pleasant. That wasn't to say she wasn't very direct, though, and not even remotely timid about voicing her opinion.

As Abby herself was on the assertive side, she found a kindred spirit in Gemma. They'd been able to work out the details for the whole event, maybe not with ease, but they'd agreed on most decisions and compromised on the rest.

At first sight this evening, Abby thought Gemma might be a

cast member from *Ponce*. The woman never looked her fifty-six years, more like thirty-six, but tonight she was especially stunning. She'd let her black hair down, and that combined with how she filled out that shimmering black dress was a rather lethal combination. It was definitely different not seeing her in business clothes.

Though the same could be said for Abby. In fact, Logan *had* said the exact same thing the night they'd spent in Mirabelle, right before he'd stripped her out of her jeans.

Well *that* was something she didn't need to be thinking about.

He'd moved on. And she would, too.

The pang in her belly was more than a little staggering and she had to take a deep breath to get past it. She was probably just hungry.

Yup, that was what it was.

"Brooke is keeping an eye on the auction." Abby turned to indicate her assistant who was standing next to her; it was the only way she could stop herself from giving Gemma a beyond forced smile in that moment.

"People are bidding left and right. The sheets are filling up with names," Brooke said as she practically bounced on her sparkly pink heels.

It was a feat to be sure to pull off the shoes and that long platinum blonde hair of hers and not look like Barbie. But Brooke's long-sleeved, off-the-shoulder, navy blue dress somehow toned down the glitz and made her look elegant.

The girl was beautiful to be sure, and Abby had a feeling that people were going to underestimate her. She was fresh out of grad school and a little naive, but she had so much potential it was ridiculous. She also had the ability to babble like it was nobody's business, but she was reining herself in tonight.

"Well, I should get in there and get my name on something I think," Gemma said, raising her eyebrows.

Abby took a deep breath, steeling herself before she headed into that room...with him.

They were just outside the ballroom when Gemma was pulled aside by a rather dashing man in a tux. He had a thick beard and long hair that brushed the back of his jacket. The streaks of gray blended subtly among all of the ebony black. He slipped his hand into Gemma's, lacing their fingers together.

"Abby, Brooke, this is my husband Dr. Alejandro Faro, head of oncology. Alejandro, this is Abby and her assistant Brooke." Gemma beamed as she waved her free hand between the two of them.

Abby had heard a lot about Alejandro, she'd just never met him. Apparently, St. Ignatius didn't have a no fraternization clause in their contracts. Lucky bastards.

Not that it mattered anymore.

Abby was pulled out of her bitterness when Alejandro reached forward and grabbed her hand. He bent his head as he kissed the back of it. "A pleasure. Gemma has told me all about you. The Stampede better be careful, otherwise I think she might steal you away for St. Ignatius."

"It's true." Gemma nodded. "They better watch out."

Brooke shot Abby a surprised look, but she was distracted—understandably so—a moment later when Alejandro bent to kiss her hand in turn.

Movement out of the corner of Abby's eye had her turning to the open doors of the ballroom. Logan came through them heading straight for her. There was a look of determination in his eyes that she'd never seen before.

Well, at least not directed at her.

"Sorry to interrupt, I was just hoping for a brief word with Ms. Fields before dinner starts."

Ms. Fields? Was he freaking kidding her? But how the hell was she supposed to say *no* and not look unprofessional?

It took everything in her to straighten her shoulders and smile up at him. "Yes." She nodded before she turned to Gemma, Alejandro, and Brooke.

She forced herself to keep that smile in place as she introduced Logan to the group.

"Oh, I know Mr. James," Gemma beamed. "He's been visiting the kids the last couple of weeks at the hospital with Mr. Kilpatrick and Mr. Fabian."

"What?" Abby's mouth dropped open.

"Yes. They were Batman, Robin, and Superman the first time. Then Captain America, Thor, and Iron Man the second time. Who will it be next, Mr. James?"

"I'm thinking the Hulk, Hawkeye, and Spider-Man. Jace thinks he can give the blue and red spandex suit justice."

All sense and logic seemed to vacate Abby's brain. Logan was dressing up as superheroes to visit sick kids in the hospital?

No, no, no. You are not *allowed to find him sweet and sexy right now.*

"Who did you dress up as?" Abby asked before she could stop herself.

"Batman and Captain America." There was a gleam in his eye that should be illegal.

God, he was infuriating. Who was this man in front of her? She was beginning to think she had no idea. He was a complete and total ass one second, bringing a date to the event tonight without telling her that whatever they had was over, and then she finds out he's been visiting sick kids in the hospital.

How the hell was she supposed to process this?

"A pleasure seeing you tonight, Gemma, and very nice to meet you, Alejandro," Logan said before he nodded to Brooke. "Ms. Fields, if you'll please?" He indicated the hallway behind them with his hand.

Abby was too stunned by the newest tidbit of information to do anything but lead him down the hallway and into an empty room.

She heard the lock click behind her as she went to reach for the switch. Just as the room was filled with light, she was pushed up against the wall.

Chapter 8

Sometimes Sharing Is *Not* Caring

Logan's mouth came down hard on Abby's, and for just a moment she forgot that she was angry with him. It just so happened that the moment involved his tongue in her mouth. Her hands were in his hair and she was kissing him back. She'd missed him way more than she'd thought...and then she remembered that he *hadn't* missed her.

"Stop." She turned her head away from him, her hands falling from his hair and going flat on his chest where she pushed at him to move away.

He didn't budge.

"Stop?" he asked. "Why? What's going on?"

She turned and looked up at him. "You tell me."

"Red, I have no idea what I'm supposed to tell you."

"Does your date know you're in here?"

"My...what?"

"Your date. The beautiful brunette that was all over you. Look, I get that we never established being exclusive, but I don't share, so whatever—"

Logan cut her off, covering her mouth again, and she couldn't stop her traitorous body from going over to it. Going over to him. Pushing him away the first time had been hard enough, and she couldn't find the strength to do it again.

She judged herself just a little in that moment. Or she would have if she hadn't been so focused on the feeling of Logan's hands on her hips. How they moved down her thighs and around to her bottom. He filled his palms and squeezed, making her groan.

He pulled back, his breath washing over her mouth as he skimmed his nose along hers. It took her a moment to open her eyes, and all she could see were Logan's looking right back at her.

"The brunette is my sister Adele, the head costume designer for *Ponce*, the TV show that you invited the cast and crew to tonight's little dinner."

"Your sister?" Her brain was slow to start. Either because of the fact that Logan's mouth was just inches from hers…or because every hard inch of him was pressing into the rest of her body.

Actually, it was probably both.

"Yes, Adele James."

Abby remembered putting the name on the list, but James was a fairly common last name. She hadn't known this was his sister.

"I…didn't know."

"You didn't know? *You?*" His eyebrows climbed up his forehead. "I didn't think that was possible. You're little Miss Attention-to-Detail."

"I knew you had a sister, not that she lived here. Or that she worked on *Ponce*. That information wasn't in the dossier I'd been given on each player when I first started the job."

"And you didn't look me up since then?"

"No, I prefer it when you tell me things like people do in normal relationships."

His head kicked back just slightly in surprise. "I don't think we have a normal relationship, Red."

"Isn't that the truth? Not telling each other about families, or going to visit sick kids in the hospital. When did that start?"

"A couple weeks after we got back from visiting Dale."

"And you got Jace and Andre involved?"

"Yeah, it's a good cause."

"You continually surprise me, Logan James," she whispered as she reached up and touched the side of his face, cradling his jaw in her hand.

He turned his head, kissing her palm. "And you continue to surprise me." His eyes went back to hers, humor flickering with the gold in a sea of green. His head tilted to the side and those lips of his quirked. "So you were jealous when you thought Adele was my date?"

"Could you be any more smug?"

"I think I could, but your dress is distracting me from it." He moved his hands from their location on her butt, traveling back to her hips and running them up to her waist before he slid them back down. "Does it make you feel any better that I can't even think straight when I look at you?"

"Maybe a little."

He grinned as he bent his head, kissing a path down her chest and dipping his tongue between her breasts. "Tell me you are wearing something lacy under this."

"My bra is. I'm not wearing any panties."

Logan's head came up in an instant. "What was that?"

"I'm going commando. The material of this dress is too thin. Shows everything. So I took a leaf out of your book."

"Come home with me tonight, Red. I'm tired of waiting for this to all die down. I need you in my bed tonight."

"Need? Really, that's—"

"Need," he cut her off, one of his hands moving down to her knee. He pulled her leg up around his waist before he pushed his palm up and underneath the hem of her dress, touching her bare skin. "You're right, we haven't established a lot of things and I think that we should. Tonight. After I strip you out of this dress." His hand moved around and he now held her bare bottom. He pulled her closer and the hard length of his erection pressed into her belly.

The predatory gleam in his eyes made her breath catch, and she felt more than a little light-headed. She held on to the lapels of his tux, needing something to keep her from sliding to the floor. Though as he still had a pretty tight grip on her ass, she figured she was okay.

"But I'm going to establish something right now." He moved his mouth to the side, kissing the hollow beneath her ear. "I don't share, either."

His hand dipped low, traveling past the curve of her bottom. He moved along her folds before he slid two fingers inside her. Her head fell back against the wall and she had to bite her lip to stop from moaning.

"And not being able to touch you these last few weeks? Not being able to have you when I *need* you?"—he emphasized the word *need* with a light nip to her skin—"that's unacceptable to me." He whispered the last few words as he moved his fingers in and out of her. "Do you have any idea how desperately I want to bury myself inside you right now? But I can't, because I know that once I start I won't be able to stop. And we only have minutes."

Minutes? She wasn't sure she was going to need that long. She'd been pretty desperate for him, too, and she couldn't stop herself from thrusting against his hand, seeking more pressure.

"Logan, *please.*" The words came out of her mouth strangled and breathy, which was good because it meant she wasn't screaming them.

"What do you think I'm trying to do?" His other hand moved between their bodies and quickly went to the apex of her thighs, where he started to work her clit with his fingers.

The double onslaught was more than she should take, and she started coming, bucking against his hands as she cried out. Logan's mouth covered hers, muffling the sound. He brought her down nice and slow with soft strokes of his tongue on hers, and his fingers that were still expertly moving between her legs.

"We're going to have to finish this tonight," he said against her mouth, his lips brushing hers. "In my bed."

"Yes." She nodded.

He kissed her one last time before he pulled his hand out from under her dress, straightening it before he took a step back and looked her up and down.

"Damn," he said as he shook his head. "I have no idea how I'm going to make it through the night with you looking like this."

Her eyes darted to the mirror over his shoulder. Her flushed reflection and bright blue eyes stared back. At least he hadn't messed up her hair.

Thank God for small favors.

"Crap, how am I supposed to go out there like this?"

"You?" he asked, incredulous. "I think I have a more pressing problem."

Her eyes traveled down the front of his pants to where his erection was clearly straining against his zipper.

"And whose fault is that? You're the one who dragged me in here."

He reached forward, pulling her from the wall and into his hard body. "I had to get my point across."

"Oh, I think you were successful with that," she said as she cupped the front of his pants.

"Red, I don't suggest you start something unless you intend on finishing it." He raised his eyebrows as he grabbed her hand and pulled it away.

"Well, aren't you a fine one to talk?"

"Uh, I think you finished nicely."

"Hmm, that's very true." She held on to his lapels again as she stretched up and placed a kiss to his mouth. When she pulled back she attempted to straighten him out, but he still looked pretty unrumpled considering she'd been holding on to him for dear life. "What you do to a three-piece suit should be illegal."

"The same could be said about you in this dress. You look stunning tonight, Red."

His words made her breath catch for an entirely different reason than it had earlier. "Thank you."

"I can't keep my eyes off you, and I really wish I didn't have to take me hands off you. But I suppose we should get back out there."

"Yes. We should."

"I'm going to need a minute to catch my breath. Probably shouldn't walk out together anyway; I don't think I could hide anything at the moment. But if anyone asks about your cheeks, just say that we got into an argument."

"About?"

"I'm sure you'll come up with something. You always do."

"I'll see you out there when you get yourself"—she gestured to the front of his pants—"under control."

"Could take a while."

She grinned as she pulled away from him and headed for the door. But before she could open it, Logan put his hand over the exit. She turned to look at him over her shoulder, but he spun her around all the way and pushed her back into the solid wood.

"Just one more," he said as he lowered his mouth to hers. Thank God for smudge-proof lipstick.

* * *

The next three hours went by in a rush. Abby worked her way around the room, thanking everyone she could for coming, introducing the players to the guests, and making sure the silent auction was running smooth.

Waiters circled around with trays of drinks, and the dance floor was filled with couples who moved in time with the music. She wished she could go out there with Logan. Wished she could press her body to his, rest her head against his chest while he wrapped his arms around her.

Her gaze wandered to the other side of the room, where she spotted him with Jace and Andre. They all had drinks in their hands and were smiling as they talked to two women in floor-length gowns.

Not for the first time, she resented the fact that they had to keep their relationship a secret. But it was what she'd signed up for. If she wanted to be with him, she was just going to have to deal with it.

"So you're the infamous Red?"

Abby turned and looked up at the rather statuesque Adele

James. A tiny diamond stud glinted from the left side of her nose, and the streaks of red in her dark brown hair were expertly curled in just the right way to highlight the color.

"Adele James." She reached out, holding her hand in front of Abby. She had a tattoo of a threaded needle and a stitched heart over her right wrist.

"Abby Fields," Abby said as she grabbed Adele's outstretched hand and shook it.

"I believe you know my brother, Logan James." Her shrewd eyes zeroed in and she did a quick assessment of Abby before she nodded her head in approval, her mouth quirking to the side.

There was no *believe* about it. Adele knew exactly who Abby was. So Logan hadn't been exactly tight-lipped when it came to her. That was enlightening. So was the fact that it appeared she hadn't been found wanting.

A waiter came up to them, offering some champagne. Both women took a glass before he smiled and moved off.

"I was told you were the mastermind behind this whole event."

"Mastermind? That's high praise."

"It is. And my brother doesn't tend to give praise where it isn't due."

"That so?" Abby asked, raising her eyebrows.

"Yes, so I know it's well earned by those he gives it to," Adele said before she took a sip of her drink.

Never in Abby's life had she been given *the talk*. She'd given it many times. Had given it to her stepfather when he started dating her mom, had given it to Brendan when he started dating Paige. So the fact that it was coming from Logan's little sister was more than a little interesting.

"I'm sure you've picked up on the fact that he's a bit of a private person."

"*A bit*?" Abby almost snorted.

"Yes, a bit." Adele's mouth twitched in amusement as she turned and focused on the group of men across the room. Two other women had joined them, and the uneven numbers made Abby feel slightly antsy. "My brother can be hard to get to know sometimes…hard to work with. But him being cooperative? Well, it isn't small potatoes."

"I've picked up on that actually."

Adele looked back to Abby, but this time a full-blown smile turned up the corners of her mouth. "Good."

Abby had the feeling that she was just granted approval by one Adele James.

Well, wasn't that something?

Both women returned their gazes to the men just as one of the newcomers around them, this one in a low-cut silver gown with a slit up the side, reached out and touched Logan's arm. Her palm slid up his sleeve until she got to his bicep, where she wrapped her fingers around him and held on.

It didn't matter that Abby knew she was going home with him. Didn't matter that the smile on his mouth was forced. Didn't matter that there was no heat in his eyes as he looked at the blonde who had her hand on him.

For the second time that night, the jealously that ran through Abby was overwhelming. She knew nothing was going to happen with Blondie over there, but it didn't change the fact that she couldn't be the one with her hands on Logan. That she couldn't stake her claim. Let all of the women in the room *know* that he was hers.

That he was hers? Where the hell had that come from?

"I wouldn't worry about that." Adele's voice dropped low so that there was no chance she could be overheard.

No sooner were the words out of Adele's mouth than a waiter passed by the group. Logan managed to move away from Blondie's touch as he grabbed two glasses of champagne. He handed one to the woman, and as her other hand was wrapped around her satin clutch, she was now unable to touch him.

Well, wasn't he clever?

His eyes came up for just a second and he focused on Abby. Even though they were on opposite ends of the room, she felt the heat like his hands had just passed over her body. He winked at her, his mouth kicking up into a grin as he looked between her and his sister.

"Jace was right," Adele whispered in amazement.

"Huh?" Abby turned, forcing herself to pull her eyes away from Logan. If they continued to look at each other like that, their secret relationship wouldn't be much of a secret anymore.

"He said that Logan smiles more. I haven't seen that look on his face in…" A sadness flickered in her gaze before she glanced over to her brother. "A long time. Logan is definitely a one-woman kind of guy. Unlike his friend over there." The touch of bitterness in Adele's statement was hard to miss even in her whisper.

Abby found herself automatically looking over to the group again. She was going to give herself whiplash at this rate.

Her eyes ran around the circle, taking in the three men. Andre was married, so Abby sure hoped Adele was talking about Jace. But before she could say anything on the matter, Jace's hand came up and he ran it across the back of the brunette in the short green dress.

"Typical," Adele muttered under her breath.

Abby turned just in time to see Adele's nostrils flare as she looked away from the group. She took a deep breath right before she let it out in a frustrated sigh.

Abby was beyond curious as to what *that* had been about. Before she could even open her mouth to say anything, though, Adele nudged her arm and indicated a spot across the room with her chin.

Kent Proctor was surrounded by a group of people, mostly women. The one at the center, and who he was focusing on the most? Felicity Carter, the lead actress on *Ponce*.

"What is she doing?" Adele asked, shaking her head. "She should know better."

"You friends with her?"

"Yes. She's a good girl. A bit naive, obviously, as she's talking to that asshat. I heard about what he said to you. That was uncalled for."

Abby hadn't spoken to Proctor since the whole locker room incident. Her bosses had removed her from any and all things that had to do with him. She wasn't upset by any means that she no longer had to deal with him, but she got the feeling that they blamed her a little bit for the incident.

Proctor had become Dingle's problem since the two seemed to have an amicable relationship.

Birds of a feather.

They had a lot in common. Proctor was much like Dingle in the essence that he could be considered attractive, that is, until his personality came to light. He opened his mouth and arrogance spewed forth like vomit. He had long light blond hair that he slicked back and blue eyes that revealed absolutely nothing of the man that lay beneath them.

There was just something about him that put her on edge.

"Maybe we should go save her."

Adele looked over at Abby and shook her head. "You won't be doing anything. My brother sees you anywhere near that guy, and you will have a situation much worse than what happened in that locker room. You should know Logan only loses it like that when it comes to people he cares about."

"He...what?"

Okay, so he'd told her he *needed* her earlier that evening. He'd told her he didn't share, that he wanted to establish things about their relationship. She knew all that, yes, but there was something about somebody else knowing it. About hearing it come out of the mouth of someone who knew him.

It was...unsettling.

"Calling it like I see it. Now if you'll excuse me, I have a friend to save," Adele said before she headed across the room, leaving Abby just a little bit dumbfounded.

Chapter 9

Established

Limos had been hired for all the players that night, so there was no chance of anyone drinking and driving. Logan had called his driver and asked him to pull around to the back so that he and Abby could slip in unnoticed.

The driver had barely pulled away from the curb before they were both reaching for each other. Abby straddled Logan and settled herself expertly on his lap, but he made sure the privacy partition was fully closed before he pushed the hem of her dress up her legs.

He gripped her bare thighs as he leaned back in the seat and looked up at her, watching as she first removed his bow tie. She made quick work of the buttons on his vest, then his shirt, her palms skimming across his bare skin when she had all of them undone.

It felt like forever since she'd had her hands on him and he savored the moment; he also took the time to appreciate the fact that *he* could touch *her*. His hands moved to her hips, pushing her dress farther up her body.

He dropped his gaze to the apex of her thighs where he admired her panty-less state, the way her bare flesh looked against his black pants. But he didn't get that long to admire the sight as she took that moment to rub herself against the bulge pressing against the front of said pants.

His head fell back against the seat and he closed his eyes, trying to calm his breathing. It had been way too long—too long for him, that is—since he'd been inside her. And having her grinding against him was almost more than he could take.

Almost. But not quite.

Her mouth came down hard on his as she continued to move over him. She thrust her tongue past his lips and he let her in immediately, tasting the sweetness of her mouth. She nipped at his bottom lip, her teeth biting into the flesh with just enough pressure to cause a sting.

"Condom?" she whispered against his mouth.

"Wallet. Jacket pocket."

She pulled back from him, slipping her hand into the folds of fabric that she'd pushed to the side of his chest. When she withdrew her hand a moment later she held his black leather wallet in her hand. She opened it and withdrew the small square package before she threw the wallet on the seat next to them.

She put the package between her lips before she rose just slightly and reached for the front of his pants. He could barely hear the snick of the zipper over the pounding of his blood in his ears.

All he could do was watch as she pulled him free, her hand wrapping around his dick as she stroked him from base to tip. He bucked in her grip, unable to stop himself from the full-body reaction she managed to bring out of him always.

She let go of him a moment later, smiling as she pulled the condom from between her lips. Her tongue darted out, moistening that plump mouth of hers.

She opened the package and was working the latex down him

a second later. It took everything in him not to buck again. He only had the one condom, and if it ripped he'd surely die if he couldn't get inside of her soon.

But he didn't have to wait very long. She was reaching up a second later, grabbing his shoulders as she shifted forward on his lap. She looked into his eyes as she ever so slowly sank down onto his waiting cock. The moans that filled the back of the dark limo mingled together in the small space. His long and low. Hers short and breathy.

He didn't have time to remove her dress, but as he needed one of her breasts in his mouth he unzipped the back just enough so he could pull the straps down her arms. He found red lace, *magic* red lace that pushed her breasts together. He had no other choice but to bury his face in the plumped-up perfection as he made quick work of the hooks in the back.

The second he pulled the bra from her body his lips were wrapped around one of those pretty pink nipples of hers. Her hands were in his hair, her nails scoring the back of his head.

He grabbed on to her hips again, holding on to her while she rode him. *Hard.*

"Logan." His name on her lips was a plea, and he pulled his mouth from her breast.

She looked down into his eyes as she continued to move over him. Her hair was a mess, the curls gone and the strands tangled from his hands. The lights that shone in through the windows reflected in her eyes, making them sparkle in the dark. Her unsteady breaths mingled with his and her breasts bounced in his face as she moved up and down on his lap.

He let go of her hip with one of his hands, reaching up and spearing his fingers through her hair, bringing her lips to his. He claimed her mouth, their tongues twisting together.

It was about a minute later when she pulled free from him, her head falling back on her shoulders when her orgasm hit. She screamed his name to the ceiling. She was still pulsing around him when he moved, laying her flat on the backseat.

He sat up just enough to pull his jacket and shirt from his body, throwing them on the floor of the limo before he settled back between her thighs. Her legs came up, wrapping around his waist, and her heels dug into the small of his back.

He planted his feet on the door behind him, using it for leverage as he thrust into her. His pounding hips pushed her body across the leather seats. Her hands disappeared from his head and she reached up behind her, her palms going flat on the door to hold her steady. He buried his face in her neck, nipping at her skin and soothing the spot with his tongue.

"Oh God, oh God, oh God," she moaned.

"One more."

"I can't." She shook her head frantically from side to side, her hair tickling his cheek.

"You can. One. More." He ground out the words through clenched teeth. He was going to crack a fucking molar. Almost thirty years of playing hockey and he hadn't lost any teeth, but he was going to lose them from sex with Abby.

He didn't stop pounding into her, their bodies slicked with sweat despite the constant steam of air from the vents around them.

And then her body bucked up hard.

Once.

Twice.

Three times before she was screaming his name again. Her back arched up off the seat as she started to pulse around him, squeezing his cock tight.

And this time he let himself go over to it, gave in to the building pressure at the base of his spine. His foot kicked out hard against the door as he came, his own shout of *Red* filling the back of the limo.

He meant to pull away—he really did—not wanting to crush her under his body. But her legs were still wrapped around his waist like a vice. When he tried to loosen her hold she just tightened around him, her arms moving from their stretched position above her head as she wrapped them around his shoulders.

"No." She shook her head as she ran her hands up his spine. "Stay. I need to feel you. Just for a minute longer."

"I don't want to hurt you."

"You won't," she whispered. She reached up, running her hand across his jaw, her thumb rasping his beard. "You won't hurt me."

As his arms were shaking, he had no other choice but to lower himself onto her. He had no idea if it was more from the aftereffects of the sex, or the woman who was currently in his arms.

He'd wager it was a fifty-fifty split.

* * *

Abby shifted from foot to foot as she stared out of Logan's floor-to-ceiling windows that looked out into his backyard. The lights around his pool were on, lighting up the water that moved in the steady breeze.

He had a modest house for a millionaire sports star. It wasn't one of those massive, modern monstrosities that tended toward the monochromatic side. No, his was filled with warmth. Soft leather couches with cushy pillows and blankets, thick rugs spread out across the hardwood floors, and sage drapes hanging from the windows.

She reached out, rubbing the fabric between her fingers, and she caught Logan's reflection behind her. He was standing at the bar, pouring an amber liquid from a crystal decanter into two tumbler-sized glasses.

He'd pulled his white button-up shirt back on, but his tux jacket—front pocket stuffed with his bow tie—and vest were draped over the back of the couch. His shirt hung loose over his black pants, the top three buttons undone. It was infinitely less wrinkled than her red dress, which had creases that she knew were never going to come out.

But as she'd worn the dress for him, she wasn't going to argue with the results.

He looked up, catching her gaze in the glass. The smile that broke out across his face was contagious and she turned to face him, her hands moving up and down her arms, more for something to do than anything else.

She wasn't cold by any means. Her face was still flushed from their limo rendezvous, and she had a feeling she wasn't going to be cooling down at all tonight. Especially not with the way Logan was looking at her.

She hadn't been nervous in the car. Hadn't been nervous when his mouth had found hers, when he was moving under her, over her, inside of her. No, she never had any problems with him when they were having sex.

But they were supposed to talk tonight. About their relationship.

Why, *why*, was that so terrifying to her?

But as she looked at him, watched him as he grabbed both glasses from the bar and made his way across the room, she realized it was thrilling as well.

Somewhere in the time they'd been spending together, things had changed. Morphed into something...*more*. She hadn't noticed it, not until she'd been forced to stay away from him. Not until she walked into that room tonight and thought he'd come with somebody else. Not until she'd felt that burning jealousy, that sinking disappointment.

And then he'd fixed it. Told her that he *needed* her. That word kept repeating itself over, and over, and over in her head. No one had ever said they needed her before, not in this capacity.

So yeah, equal parts terrified and thrilled.

Logan stopped in front of her, handing her a glass before he held his in the air. "To establishing things."

She smiled as she clinked her glass to his. They both brought their glasses to their mouths and took a sip. Abby knew it was scotch immediately. She let it sit in her mouth for just a moment before she swallowed. It burned her throat.

Just what she needed, something to make her even hotter.

"Macallan. Nice," she said before she put her nose over the liquid and sniffed, closing her eyes for just a second and letting the aroma take her to good memories.

"You know your scotches."

Her eyes opened and she found him watching her, an impressed look on his face. "My stepdad is a whiskey drinker, scotch specifically. So I know a few things beyond a bottle of Jack Daniel's."

Logan grinned. "Ain't nothing wrong with a bottle of Jack. Shouldn't really play drinking games with this," he said, holding the glass in the air before he took another sip.

"That would be a pretty expensive game."

"Yeah, especially when I know I don't have to get you drunk to get you naked." He took a step forward, his hand sliding across her hip and to her back as he pulled her into his body.

"No, you don't." She looked up at him.

"And what about the truth? Do I have to get you drunk for that?" He leaned down, opening his mouth over hers.

She parted her lips instantly, letting him in. The scotch tasted so much better on his tongue. Logan James, his own personal vintage. Aged thirty-two years to perfection.

"Truth," he said against her mouth. "What do you want us to be?" He pulled back just slightly and looked down into her eyes.

"I want it to be exclusive."

"I thought we already established that part. No sharing, remember?" He shook his head. "Well, unless it's with each other. Like beds, and showers, and pizza."

"Okay. So what's next?"

"Is there anything you'd like to change?"

"About how we've been doing things?"

"Yes." He nodded.

"More than I can count. But we can't change them."

"Why?" he asked as his eyebrows bunched together. "Who says?"

"I hate that I can't touch you in public." She put her hand on his neck before she ran her palm down to his chest. "That you can't touch me. I wish I could've danced with you tonight. Wish that this didn't have to be a secret." Her voice dropped at the end to just above a whisper.

"I wish that, too," he said as he put his hand over hers, pulling it off his chest and up to his mouth. He placed a kiss to the inside of her palm before he dropped it and pulled back. He grabbed the glass from her other hand, setting both crystal tumblers on the table next to them.

"Dance with me, Abby?" he asked as he held out his hand.

"Yes."

She slipped her hand into his, their fingers lacing together as he led her to the other side of the room. He hit a button on the stereo and music filled the air. The deep rich voice of a woman, slightly husky as she sang about a love that could never be torn apart.

He spun her slowly before he pulled her into his body, his free hand landing on the small of her back. She rested her head on his chest and closed her eyes as he guided her through the room.

"When this first started with us, I thought it was so simple," he whispered close to her ear. "It was perfect really. What could be so complicated about a secret relationship?"

She tilted her head back so she could look up into his eyes.

"But as it turns out, it ended up being a lot more complicated than I originally planned." He pressed his lips to hers in a light kiss. Their mouths barely touched but it didn't stop the desire that coursed through her.

This was how it was. All the freaking time.

"So what do we do now that we're here?" she asked, trying to focus on something besides his hand that was moving up and down her spine in a slow, tantalizing journey. "Now that it's apparent this is more than just sex."

"We figure it out."

"You keep saying that."

He stopped dancing as his hand moved from her back, and he reached up to cradle the side of her face. "That's the only thing I know, because the other option isn't a possibility."

"And what's the other option?"

"Letting you walk away." This time when he kissed her it was not sweet, it was all-consuming.

Possessing.

She belonged to him.

She loved him.

Chapter 10

Sins of the Father

Logan ran his hands through Abby's hair, twirling a strand around his finger. She loved it when someone played with her hair, such a simple thing that for her was beyond special.

Every time the pads of his fingers touched her scalp, a fresh wave of goose bumps broke out over her skin. His other hand was in hers and she traced the lines on his palm, her fingers just lightly brushing his skin.

Their bodies made a sideways T. Her head resting against his stomach and using it as a pillow as she stretched out across the width of his California king bed. Whenever he laughed her head bounced lightly.

She'd pulled on one of his worn Stampede T-shirts, faded beyond reason—the black now gray—and a hole in the collar. The only thing he was wearing was a sheet, which rested just below his hips, and her hair that was spread across his chest.

This was the position they'd been in for hours now, asking each other question after question.

She now knew that he'd started skating when he was three.

"I fell flat on my face. But I got up immediately."

That he'd shared a room with his younger brother Liam growing up.

"I still don't know how we didn't kill each other."

That he had an unhealthy obsession with *Archie Comics.*

"When my parents sold their house and moved, my mother made me take every last one. I have four massive storage bins filled with them in my garage."

She listened as he talked about his family. How proud he was of his brother and sister for following their dreams, no matter how unconventional. How happy he was for his parents for doing what they wanted and traveling like they'd always talked about.

Abby talked to him about growing up in Philadelphia. Told him all about Paige, who was more of a sister than a best friend. Told him all about her few years spent in D.C. and how happy she was to get out of there. She went into great detail about her mother Naomi and stepfather Matthew Clark.

Abby was eighteen when Naomi started a relationship with Matt, so Abby had never really looked at him as a father figure. But she did genuinely like the guy. He loved her mother, and he'd always been good to Abby. That was all that really mattered, right?

"So Matt is the one who taught you about whiskey?"

"Yes, he is a bit of a connoisseur. My mom hates the stuff. I liked it okay so I'd indulge him whenever I visited, and I ended up acquiring a taste for it."

"You mean beyond the shots of Jack?" he asked. She could hear the smile in his voice.

But where it was easy to talk about her mother and Matt, she'd glossed over the topic of her father. What was she supposed to say beyond the fact that Jim Fields had picked up his life in Philadelphia and left Abby and her mother? Moved away when she was ten years old.

Visits with him had been few and far between, and those ended on a sour note. He'd actually called her the day before, but she was so busy dealing with the charity dinner she let it go to voice mail. She simply ignored anything that had to do with her father yesterday. But the red dot on her smartphone indicating voice mail had been glaring at her ever since.

She wasn't ready to listen to it. Though, she was never ready for anything that pertained to her father.

There'd been a moment, when Logan had asked about Abby's first broken heart, that her tracing pattern on Logan's hand had faltered.

The truth? Her first broken heart had been from her father. But she wasn't ready to share that yet.

"I was fourteen. His name was Clip Summers."

"Clip? Sounds like an asshat."

"He was that," she said, nodding, the unsettling feeling in her stomach blooming.

She'd lied to Logan, and the words tasted like acid coming out of her mouth.

* * *

Abby had been sitting alone in the restaurant for thirty minutes.

Thirty. *Freaking.* Minutes.

She reached forward and grabbed her glass of sauvignon blanc and finished it off before she looked over and caught the eye of the waiter. The smile on her mouth was forced as she held the empty glass up in the air. He nodded to her before he headed to the bar.

She did *not* want to be here. Not in any way, shape, or form. Not at this table. Not at this restaurant. Not in this city.

The Stampede were in the middle of a weeklong stint of games on the road. Their current location: Pittsburgh, Pennsylvania. Abby was not a fan of the city. Actually, that was a bit of an understatement.

She hated Pittsburgh, had for the last nineteen years. It wasn't the city's fault that her feelings were far less than positive. The *city* had done nothing to offend her...except for the fact that it was where her father lived.

When she was younger she'd been naive with her visits to her father, thinking that her time here would involve the two of them doing things together.

She'd been wrong.

So. *Damn.* Wrong.

She'd done more with her various babysitters than she ever did with her father, and being back here opened all those wounds afresh.

So yeah, she despised the city and all things associated with it. The Stampede better freaking crush the Penguins tomorrow.

This was why her father had called her the week before; he'd seen that the team would be in town, and he wanted to have dinner with her. For some reason she didn't quite understand, she'd said yes.

Apparently that little girl from so long ago was still desperate for a little attention from the one man who *should* be guaranteed to love her. And that little girl wasn't going to give up hope, even when she was under the scornful eye of the cynical twenty-nine-year-old who knew her father was just going to disappoint her.

Again.

Then there was the fact that she always felt like she was betraying her mother whenever she saw her dad. But guilt was something her mother had never made her feel when it came to this.

Not once. Not ever.

But Naomi was a better woman, a *stronger* woman, than most. She'd been devastated when Jim left, but she'd gotten over that—and him—years ago. Long before she met Matt. Abby wished she could figure out how to heal this wound, because walking around with so much pain was pointless. Her father didn't care, so why should she?

Abby was pulled out of her thoughts as the waiter returned with a fresh glass of wine, setting it on the table before he took a step back and eyed the empty seats.

"Do you know what your two guests would like to drink?" he asked.

"Guest. And he should be here soon," she said as she glanced down at her phone to check her text messages.

Nope. Nothing from her dad. But when had her time ever been important to him? The most recent message was from Logan. He'd sent it about ten minutes ago asking what time she'd be back to the hotel.

It had been seven days since the charity dinner. Seven days since they'd reestablished themselves and had started to open up way more than either of them had before.

They'd text each other throughout the day playing *Truth*. Most of the things ridiculous like favorite ice cream flavor (hers turtle tracks, his rocky road) or favorite movie (hers *Benny & Joon*, his *Star Wars: A New Hope*). The more serious *Truths* were reserved for when they were in bed, wrapped up in each other. There they talked about their biggest regrets, their passions, things that shaped them.

Well, some of the things…

Abby had yet to tell Logan about her father. The damage he'd caused. The scars that would never go away. She hated it. Hated feeling so weak, and that was something she didn't want Logan to see.

She wasn't ready for it.

Which was why she hadn't been *exactly* truthful about tonight. She'd just told him she had a dinner meeting and that she'd be free afterward. She had a feeling she was going to need something to distract her after this. And Logan definitely fit that bill.

"The reservation was made for three. A Mr. and Mrs. Fields, and guest. I'm sure they'll be here soon." He eyed the two chairs again not so subtly before he moved off.

Her father had said nothing about anyone else joining them. Who would he be bringing along? He'd said he wanted dinner with his family.

Family. He had no idea what that word meant.

Abby found herself reaching for her glass of wine before she even realized it. She took a healthy sip before she set it down, and as her eyes landed on the front door she wanted to grab the glass again and chug it.

Crush it in one fell swoop.

Her father *was* bringing a guest. A woman with pin-straight blonde hair, a full mouth that was the perfect example of what women wanted when they went to a plastic surgeon, and high cheekbones. Abby couldn't see the rest of her as her rain-spotted Burberry trench coat was covering the rest of her body, but her sapphire blue Manolo Blahniks were stunning.

Too bad the woman's excellent taste in shoes had no hope of endearing her to Abby. It wasn't a possibility as she was currently arm in arm with Abby's father.

She hadn't seen him in three years, but to her he always looked the same.

Jim Fields was and always had been a handsome man. He

looked like Richard Gere, the 2002 model when Mr. Gere had done the movie *Chicago*. Salt-and-pepper gray hair, though more on the salt side.

He was fifty-three and Abby would bet money that the woman he was leading to the table was younger than her own twenty-nine years.

She stood, more for something to do that anything else. Really she wanted to get the hell out of there. This had been a mistake. A horrible, *horrible,* mistake. But her feet were rooted to the ground, kind of like she was watching a train wreck and she just couldn't pull herself away.

The problem? The train wreck was her life and she was living it.

"Abby, sorry we're late," Jim said as he got closer to the table. "Lacey was having trouble picking out something to wear." He turned, giving the blonde on his arm an indulgent smile.

"Lacey." Abby said the name slowly; it was the only way to keep the bitterness out of her voice…or most of the bitterness anyway.

But none of that mattered because a second later Abby had to use every ounce of her willpower to not completely and totally lose her shit.

Jim stepped behind Lacey, grabbing the shoulders of her coat as she worked at the tie around her waist. When he pulled the khaki-colored material away from her it was to reveal a rather prominent baby belly stretching at the stomach of her polka-dotted dress.

As soon as Lacey's arms were free, she reached for Abby's hands, grabbing both of them and holding firm. Abby couldn't stop herself from looking down at their hands, and when she did she saw a very familiar ring glistening on the ring finger of Lacey's left hand.

Abby recognized it immediately as it had sat on her mother's hand for years. It was a Fields family heirloom, going back three generations. Naomi had given it back in the divorce, and now it was on this woman's hand.

Abby was numb. Her ears were ringing and she wasn't quite sure she remembered how to breathe. She couldn't think to save her life, which was probably why she didn't pull away when Lacey leaned forward, placing a kiss on each of her cheeks.

"It's so nice to *finally* meet you," Lacey said sweetly. "Jim talks about you all the time."

Well, if anything was going to bring Abby back to the moment, it was that.

"Oh really?" Abby's eyebrows raised up her forehead as she looked at her father who was currently pulling off his own jacket, flecks of rain clinging to the fabric and his hair.

"Of course I do." He smiled as he placed his jacket on the empty chair. Then he reached out, grabbing Abby's shoulders and pulling her in for a hug.

Her father very rarely hugged her, and it took everything in her to not pull away. Instead she just stood there, stiff as a board, until he let go and took a step back.

"Abby." He grinned, not even remotely bothered by the tension that was radiating off her. "I want you to meet your stepmom, Lacey Fields."

She wanted to run away.

* * *

The elevator doors opened onto the seventh floor and Logan stepped out, making his way down the hallway to Abby's room. He'd had practice that afternoon and then he'd gone out to dinner with Jace and Raymond Kirk.

Ray had played with Logan at the University of Michigan, and he was currently a defenseman for the Penguins. They caught up with each other whenever they had the opportunity.

After dinner Jace had left with their waitress, and after another drink with Ray, Logan headed back to the hotel. He was looking forward to spending the rest of the evening with Abby.

He pulled the keycard out of his pocket and slid it in the slot. The light turned green and he stepped inside.

The room was dim, the only light coming from a small lamp in the corner and the steady flickering from the TV. One of those fashion-design reality TV shows was playing. He recognized the show immediately because it was the same one Adele watched religiously.

The bed was blocked by the wall, and when it came into view he found Abby sitting up, her back against the headboard and her legs folded in front of her on the bed. She was wearing leggings and a stampede T-shirt, the collar artfully ripped out so that one side hung low, exposing her bare shoulder. A pile of papers was stacked in her lap, a glass of wine in her hand. She took a sip before she set the wineglass on the nightstand.

"Hey." He tossed his jacket on the chair in the corner as he made his way into the room.

"Hey," she said softly, a small smile on her lips.

He couldn't see her eyes, the glare from the TV reflecting off her reading glasses, so he wasn't sure if it was a tired smile or a sad one...or both. Whatever it was, there was something that told him she wasn't okay at the moment.

"How was dinner?" she asked as she gathered the papers in her lap. She unfolded her legs and stood, walking across the room to the desk in the corner.

"Good," he said as he slipped off his shoes. He watched her as he loosened his tie, her shoulders rigid as she put her paperwork away. "It was nice catching up with Ray. What about you? How was your dinner meeting?"

She stopped for just a second, and the tension in her shoulders moved down her back.

"Fine," she said with a nod before she unzipped her bag and slid the folder inside.

Yeah, he wasn't buying that for a second. Besides the fact that she was wound so tight he thought she might snap any second now, he really hated that she wouldn't look at him.

He crossed the room, coming behind her and putting his hands on her waist. He turned her around, pulling off her glasses as he looked down into her face. He was more than slightly staggered by the pain he found in her eyes.

"What's wrong?"

"Nothing to worry about." Her chin dipped, her eyes leaving his as she reached up and fiddled with the top button on his shirt.

"Red," he whispered as he touched her chin, lightly pushing up until he had her eyes again. "Truth: what's going on?"

"I thought there were two other options with that game."

"Not tonight." He shook his head. "Just the one."

"But I have wine." She gestured to the nightstand behind him, giving him another weak smile that failed miserably in covering up the pain etched in her eyes.

He had a feeling that wasn't her first glass, either. There was color in her cheeks, and as far as he knew only three things did that to her fair complexion: alcohol, sex, and anger. As he'd just gotten back it wasn't number two, and as she didn't appear to be angry so much as hurt, he discounted number three as well.

"Abby, talk to me." He reached up and touched her temple

before he ran his fingers down the side of her face, cupping her jaw.

"It wasn't a business dinner that I went to tonight," she said thickly.

"Then what was it?"

She swallowed hard before she cleared her throat. "A dinner with my father."

She pulled her head away from his touch, her eyes leaving his. He was just about to reach for her again when she took a step into him, burying her face in his chest. Her shoulders shook lightly and hot tears soaked into the fabric of his shirt.

He reached down, grabbing her thighs and pulling her up. Her arms slid around his shoulders and she pressed her face into his neck, her uneven breaths washing over his skin. He walked over to the bed and sat down, Abby now straddling his lap. He ran his hands up and down her back as they both settled into the new position.

She hadn't really talked about her father, and the absence of information had been obvious to him. He hadn't pried, knowing she would reveal that information when she was ready. It was how he coped with the truth about Madison, so he could provide her the same courtesy.

But the lack of information, and how she was reacting at the moment, made it obvious that she and her father didn't have a good relationship. Logan had never seen her like this before, and he found it affected him more than he was prepared for.

Sure, there was nothing like a crying woman to make him feel completely and totally awful, but this was different. He was powerless as he held Abby in his arms. He just wanted to make her pain stop, and that was something he hadn't taken on in a long time. Eight years to be exact.

It took a couple of minutes for her erratic breathing to calm down and return to a steady pattern. She pressed her lips lightly to his neck before she pulled her head from his shoulder and looked at him.

"I'm sorry... I didn't mean to lose it."

"Don't apologize for that." He reached up, pushing a strand of hair that had fallen from her ponytail behind her ear. Tears clung to her lashes, those eyes of hers somehow appearing bluer than normal.

"I'm a mess."

"A beautiful mess." *His* beautiful mess. "Tell me what happened tonight."

Her eyes left his and she started fiddling with the buttons on his shirt again.

He waited for her to gather her thoughts, waited for her to get the courage to tell him. He wasn't going to rush her, because it was *her* story.

After a minute she took a deep breath and her eyes met his. "You know how people say that they don't see it coming? That they don't realize the person they're spending their life with, the person who's supposed to love them, in fact doesn't. It seems ridiculous, right? How could they not know?" Her voice dropped as she shook her head. "But my mother didn't, she didn't know, didn't know that her husband of twelve years was just coasting through his life with her. That it was all this great big facade. And I... I didn't know it, either."

She blinked and another tear trailed down her cheek.

"So he left. Left when I was ten years old. Didn't even think twice about what he was leaving behind."

The anger in Logan's stomach bubbled. He knew this story; it was similar to the one he'd gone through with Cassidy. Parents walking out on their children. Parents who failed to do what they were supposed to do.

"We weren't enough." Her voice was barely above a whisper.

"Abby, don't say that. It isn't true."

Her bottom lip started to tremble and she pulled it up between her teeth. She blinked her eyes rapidly, more tears falling as she freed her bottom lip.

"You don't understand. The reason he wanted to see me today? He wanted to introduce me to his new wife. He got remarried without even telling me. And he married a woman who's three years younger than me." She laughed bitterly and some of that sadness in her eyes was replaced with anger.

"I sat there for two hours, Logan, two hours of him going on and on about his new wife, my new *twenty-six-year-old* stepmother," she said as she put her left hand over her chest. "*And* my new baby brother. She's pregnant. Pregnant with a son my father talked about with more enthusiasm than I can ever recall him talking about me."

"Abby." He reached up and ran his fingers under her eyes.

"He kept going on and on about family, how important it was. But it wasn't important when he left nineteen years ago. *I* wasn't important when he left. I wasn't enough."

"No." He shook his head, cradling her face in both of his palms. "He's a fraction of a man. He's the one who missed out on knowing who you are. I know it's hard to see, but I promise you, you're better off. You're better off without him. You are amazing Abby Fields. From the tips of your toes to the end of your nose, and everything in between."

"Thank you." A small smile tugged at the corners of her mouth. "You're amazing, too, Logan James."

She leaned forward and pressed her lips to his. A soft and slow tangling of tongues as her hands came up, her fingers spearing in his hair, raking the back of his head.

Logan moved, rolling her to her back and laying her gently on the bed. They both scooted back across the mattress, their mouths never separating.

Their clothes fell away as they pulled at each other. Their hands roamed across every inch of the other's body as they moved together. And then he was pushing inside of her and she was clutching at his shoulders as she gasped for breath. Clutching at his shoulders as he whispered in her ear, as he told her over and over again just how worth it she was.

Chapter 11

Discoveries

The Stampede returned to Jacksonville the following night after a beyond close game, 5–4, over the Penguins. They pulled it out at the very end, scoring a goal with thirty seconds left.

They'd taken a late flight back, landing around midnight. Abby was more than groggy, having fallen asleep on the plane. When they stood to file out, Logan had been right behind her. She'd had her arms folded, holding her rain jacket close to her body. He'd slipped his hand into hers, tracing the back of her hand with his thumb as they moved forward.

Heat spread all along her body and settled nice and low in her belly.

"You okay to drive your car to my place?" he whispered in her ear.

She just nodded, no longer sleepy in the slightest.

Both of their cars were at the arena, so he followed her back to his house, the lights of his Mercedes a constant presence in her rearview mirror. The second they got there, he promptly carried her upstairs and stripped her out of her clothes.

They'd fallen asleep wrapped up in each other, but Abby woke up alone the following morning. The other side of Logan's bed empty.

She sat up, wiping the sleep from her eyes, and looked around the room. There was a note on the nightstand next to her, tucked underneath her phone.

She reached over and grabbed it, yawning as she unfolded it.

Red, went for a run. You better be here when I get back.— *Logan*

She smiled as she fell back against the pillows, her arms going wide as she stretched out in the bed.

Today promised to be a good one because she was spending it with Logan. He'd suggested going out on his boat, spending the day on the water. Her suitcase was still in the trunk of her car where she left it, because she hadn't needed it for anything last night. But over the last couple of months she'd left some things over here, like her bathing suit, a toothbrush, and some extra panties.

Speaking of which, she should probably grab a pair. She was only wearing one of his old T-shirts, her favorite one with the hole in the collar.

Logan might be all about going commando all the time, but she wasn't.

She headed over to his dresser, unsure of which drawer he'd put her stuff in. When she pulled the top one on the left open, she found socks. She was surprised to discover that the second drawer held boxer briefs, but she supposed he probably had to wear underwear during games and such.

The drawer underneath that held T-shirts and right before she closed it to move on, she caught a glimpse of bright pink paper sticking out of the corner. She was reaching for it before she even realized what she was doing, pulling it from the folds of fabric.

It wasn't a piece of paper, but a picture. Actually, a stack of pictures.

The photo on top was of Logan holding a little girl; the pink was from her dress. She was a tiny thing with chubby cheeks, long light brown hair, and green-gold eyes. Her arms were wrapped around his neck as she grinned at the camera.

She flipped the picture and looked at the back, Logan's familiar handwriting scrawled across it.

Madison's third birthday

Abby flipped to the next one. Logan was holding a bundle of bright yellow blankets, a sleeping baby wrapped snuggly in between the cotton folds. He wasn't looking at the camera, but was staring down at the child with adoration.

She flipped to the back again.

Madison James Thomas, June 4th

She went through the stack, seeing Madison riding a bike when she was four. Then a two-year-old Madison covered in spaghetti sitting in a high chair. Madison lying in a pile of Christmas paper giggling up at the camera. Madison wearing a black and white polka-dot dress, Adele wearing the exact same outfit, standing beside her while both of them blew kisses to the camera.

The next was of the little girl and an older couple Abby assumed were Logan's parents. The woman looked an awful lot like Adele and the man resembled Logan. They were building a snowman, Madison's snowsuit making her look a bit like a purple marshmallow.

And then one of Madison sitting in the lap of a man. He had Adele's dark brown hair and Logan's strong jaw. He was showing the little girl how to pluck the strings. A quick skim of the back informed her of what she already knew. He was Liam, Logan's brother.

There was no doubt in her mind that the little girl belonged to Logan. A little girl he had never mentioned. And as Abby went through the stack, her heart grew heavier with each picture.

Why? Why wouldn't he have said anything? And where was she?

But when Abby got to the last picture everything became clear.

Madison was in a hospital bed, hooked up to an IV. Though those eyes of hers looked exhausted, her smile was still just as big. She was wearing a yellow beanie with a black Michigan M on the front. Logan was sitting next to her, his arm wrapped around her shoulders while she leaned back into his chest.

And even though he was smiling, too, she could see the pain and devastation in his eyes.

Madison's fifth birthday.

There were no more photos after this.

Abby had noticed the lack of pictures in Logan's house the first time she'd been here. Sure there was art, photos of the mountains of Tennessee, trees emerging from the fog, but there were no pictures of people. No faces looking out from frames.

So many things started to click into place. Adele being so protective of her brother. Logan not giving Abby a hard time when she'd asked him to visit Dale. Logan going to visit the kids in the hospital, getting Jace and Andre to come with him. His insistence that his personal life stay private. He didn't want his daughter's death to become a spectacle.

But how was it that nobody knew about it? What happened to Madison's mother? Who was she? Why wasn't Logan still with her?

She straightened the pictures and returned them to the place she'd pulled them from. She closed the drawer, her hands resting on the wood for just a second.

Why did she feel like she'd just done something she shouldn't have? That she'd invaded his privacy? She wasn't upset that he hadn't told her about Madison. It was his business, his very *painful* business. She'd kept the damage of her father to herself until she'd been ready to tell him, so Logan was entitled to keep this to himself.

But how was she supposed to go about acting like she didn't know?

She was pulled out of her thoughts when a door closed downstairs. Her hands fell away from the wood and she moved on to the next drawer. She found her belongings stacked next to his athletic shorts and grabbed a pair of lime-green cotton panties and headed toward his bathroom.

For some reason she thought that if she found some underwear she'd be able to face him.

That was some great logic there.

Not.

* * *

Abby headed downstairs five minutes later with her brain still buzzing. The pictures kept flipping through her brain like a slide show. One after the other after the other. She reached up and rubbed at the spot over her heart. It ached in a way she associated with the death of Paige's father, Trevor.

A loss that was deep and permanent.

When she stepped off the last stair, she heard a noise in the kitchen and headed that way. She found Logan with his head sticking out of the refrigerator, bent over at the waist and his very fine ass on display. He was wearing a pair of jeans, and Abby's eyes immediately darted over to the clock on the stove.

How long had she slept? He'd said he was going for a run, but had he been back long enough to shower and change?

She moved to him automatically, needing her hands on him even more than she'd been prepared for.

"How long have you been up?" she asked, running her hands up his back.

He tensed as he straightened, and as Abby's hands reached around to his chest, she knew immediately he wasn't Logan.

She dropped her hands and moved back just as the man turned. It took her very confused brain a moment to process, but she recognized him from the pictures she'd just looked through upstairs.

Dark brown hair that was slightly shaggy and rumpled, green-gold eyes, and a strong-stubbled jaw.

"Oh. My. God." She said the words in a whisper, horrified. She'd pretty much just felt up Logan's brother.

"I don't think we've had the pleasure of meeting. You must be Red. I'm Liam." His eyes looked her over, taking in her bare legs before they darted back up and fixed on her eyes.

Logan's shirt was long enough to hit her past mid-thigh, but she wasn't wearing a bra. Thank the good Lord she'd put on panties.

"This isn't happening. Tell me this isn't happening and that I'm still asleep. Tell me this is a horrible nightmare."

His mouth quirked to the side in a manner that was very Logan, except not. "I'm sorry to tell you that it isn't." He shook his head.

She nodded as she took a step back toward the door. "Excuse me while I go die of embarrassment." She turned and ran smack into Logan's sweaty chest.

* * *

Logan reached out, grabbing Abby's shoulders and steadying her before she tripped and fell to the floor.

"What the—" His eyes took in Abby and her pants-less state before they darted to his brother, who was still standing in front of the open refrigerator.

Logan immediately stepped forward and pulled Abby behind him, blocking her from view. He was long since used to Liam popping in and out; it was one of the reasons his brother had a key to the house. It was just that there was normally a call before the popping in. Though to be fair, Logan wasn't always the best about keeping up with dates during the season.

"Did I know you were coming?"

"Last-minute gig in Savannah. Got booked for a festival when another band canceled. I was in Orlando and thought I'd stop through. Adele told me I needed to meet your new girlfriend." *Hot* he mouthed as he gave Logan a thumbs-up.

Logan just scowled. "Forget how to use a phone?"

"No, but you did. I called last night and this morning. Multiple times. No answer."

Okay, so maybe this one was on Logan. But to be fair he'd been on an airplane and then forgot to turn it on as he'd been pretty distracted through the rest of the night. And then this morning he'd been working out.

"Make yourself useful and cook breakfast. We will be right back." He turned and grabbed Abby's shoulders, guiding her out of the kitchen while still blocking her from view.

"Nice to meet you, Abby!" Liam called out after them.

"Has to be a nightmare," Abby whispered under her breath. "Has to be."

Logan had never seen her move so fast as she practically sprinted up the stairs to his bedroom. He shut the door behind them and she turned, her hands covering her cheeks as her face took on a shade of bright red.

"That didn't just happen."

"Could've been worse."

Her hands dropped and the horror turned to disbelief. "Oh, I don't think so. You missed the part where I felt him up."

"You what?" Okay, he was changing the locks.

"I thought he was you! Thank God I didn't grab his ass." Her head fell into her hands and she groaned.

He was trying not to laugh, really he was. It wasn't funny. He wasn't exactly thrilled about the fact that his brother had just seen Abby half-naked.

His *girlfriend* as Liam had called her. That made him smile.

He moved forward, pulling her hands from her face. "So is this now the most embarrassing moment of your life?"

He knew that it *had* been when she was thirteen and fallen down at some birthday party at the skating rink. She'd split her pants right open, revealing bright orange panties.

She bit down on the corner of her lip and he knew she was trying hard not to laugh. "Why is it that me being embarrassed always has to involve my underwear?"

"Look on the bright side, it would've been that much worse if you hadn't been wearing any underwear at all."

"That's the bright side?" she asked, raising her eyebrows.

He looked down, pulling the shirt up so that he could see her lime-green panties. "They look pretty bright to me," he said as he nodded.

"You aren't helping," she said, swatting his hands. The fabric fell back down and covered her thighs.

"Come on." He grabbed her hand and led her toward the bathroom. "Let's take a shower. I promise you'll feel much better afterward."

"I don't think hot water has that kind of healing power."

He let go of her hand, reached inside the shower, and turned the water on. He tested it a few times before he turned back to her.

"Red, I wasn't talking about the hot water." He stripped down before he walked back over to her, grabbed the hem of her shirt, and pulled it up and over her head. It hadn't even hit the floor before his mouth dropped to her nipple and he sucked it deep into his mouth.

Her groan echoed off the tile as her head fell back on her shoulders. His mouth let go of her nipple with a soft pop.

"By the time I'm done with you that flush on your face is going to have nothing to do with embarrassment."

And with that, he picked her up and carried her into the shower, bright green panties and all.

* * *

Logan stretched his legs out in front of him, bringing the sweaty glass of sweet tea to his mouth and taking a drink. A loud bark rent the air, pulling his gaze to the two women who stood out on the lawn and the Dalmatian that was running toward them with a ball in its mouth.

Logan's eyes ran down Abby's body, taking in her relaxed shoulders and the easy smile on her face. She'd managed to get over the whole incident that happened in the kitchen that morning.

Well, kind of. Her cheeks turned slightly pink whenever she looked Liam in the face.

After Logan's shower with her that morning, he called Adele and told her to come over, preferably with some clothes that would fit Abby. She didn't have anything to change into besides business clothes from the Stampede's week on the road, or her bathing suit that she now left at his house. He knew neither of those were an option, and as she wouldn't be leaving his house until the following morning, she needed something.

Abby and Adele were in no manner built the same way. His sister had gotten the height gene like the rest of the James family. She came in at five-foot-nine, and though both women were curvy, Abby's hourglass figure had a few more minutes than Adele's.

But because Adele had a wardrobe for about ten people in the many closets of her house, she found something that worked—a long dress that cinched around the waist and stretched down to the ground. Adele had hemmed it quickly when she got to Logan's, telling a protesting Abby she could keep the outfit because it looked better on her.

To say that Logan was a fan of Abby in the dress would be an understatement. It was red, so of course he liked it. The straps at her shoulders were only a few inches thick, and it dipped just low enough in the front and the back.

Katharine Hepburn, Adele's Dalmatian—a gift from Logan and Liam two Christmases ago—dropped the ball in Abby's hand. She took it before she bent over and rubbed the dog's head enthusiastically.

"Red fits right in," Liam said from the chair next to Logan.

"She does." Logan nodded. She fit right into his life almost immediately. And wasn't that a bit of a scary thought?

"She's different from any other woman I've seen you with."

Logan's gaze shifted from the women and he turned to look

at his brother. "How so?" he asked as his eyebrows rose up his face.

Liam finished off his own glass of tea, the ice cubes clinking as he put it down on the table. He leaned back in his chair as he studied Logan from behind his aviator glasses.

"She's…real."

Logan didn't need to ask what his brother meant by that. Both the women and the relationships he'd been in lately had been superficial to say the least. All surface. Nothing of real substance. That was the only way he could do it.

But Abby? Well, she was substance all right.

"There's this look in your eyes," Liam continued. "A small piece of happiness. Which is something I haven't seen in eight years."

Logan looked away from his brother, his gaze landing on Abby again. The wind shifted, blowing the skirt of her dress around the back of her legs. Her auburn hair was thrown up in a messy bun on top of her head, she wasn't wearing an ounce of makeup, and her bare feet were peeking through the blades of grass.

He was hard pressed to decide if he thought she looked more stunning in this moment than she had the night of the charity dinner in a very different red dress.

Red.

It always came back to that color. Her red hair that spread out across the pillows while she slept. Her red lipstick that made him crave to taste her mouth. Her red lace that she wrapped herself in while wearing those red heels on Valentine's Day…

Valentine's Day. The night when everything changed. The night when he fell in love with her.

Love? No, no, no.

Where the *hell* had that come from?

Logan pulled his gaze from Abby, his throat constricting and making it difficult for him to breathe.

That was... that was *way* too fucking soon.

His mouth went dry, so he brought his glass to his lips and tried to take a drink, but his throat wasn't working and he choked on the tea.

Liam did a double take between Abby and Logan. "Fuck man, really?" Liam asked, raising his eyebrows as he shifted in his seat.

"Shut up, it isn't anything to worry about."

"Bullshit. You look like you're about to hit the ground running. I just wonder if it's going to be toward something or away from it."

"I said don't worry about it."

"Uh-huh," Liam shook his head, disbelief clear.

Yeah, well, he could wonder all he wanted, because Logan had no fucking clue.

Chapter 12

Challenged

Abby stared at her computer screen for a full five minutes, the cursor blinking in the document waiting for her to finish the sentence.

Daughter, Madison James Thomas, died age five from...

But she couldn't finish the sentence, couldn't bring herself to type the words. Not from a lack of information, because she knew exactly how Logan's daughter had died.

She'd read the obituary three times.

Madison James Thomas, of Detroit, Michigan, lost her battle after six months of fighting Acute Myeloid Leukemia (AML). It was exactly a week after her fifth birthday and she was surrounded by family when she died. She was a brave little girl who was quick to smile even on her worst days of treatment...

That was the part where Abby's vision had started to blur the first time she read it. The burning at the corner of her eyes couldn't be stopped, nor could the tears that started to pool there. The article had gone on to say all the things the little girl loved: riding the bike her grandparents bought her, making her favorite dessert of s'mores with her father, helping her aunt come up with clothing designs, and singing songs with her uncle.

There was no mention about Madison's mother. Nothing about the woman baking cookies with her daughter, reading her bedtime stories, or teaching her how to swim. No, all of those stories were attached to Logan or some member of his family.

Where was this woman when Madison was growing up? Where was she when her daughter was dying?

Abby didn't know the answers to those questions, but she did know the name of Madison's mother: Cassidy Thomas. It had been on Madison's death certificate in Logan's file.

After the charity dinner Abby realized that the *complete* dossiers on the Stampede players weren't complete at all, as was evident by the fact that Adele James working for a major TV show wasn't in Logan's file. Most of the files hadn't been updated since each player joined the team, and that hadn't been done properly in the first place.

Abby had asked Brooke to do comprehensive background checks on all the players a week ago, and the folders with that information had been sitting in a stack on Abby's desk when she walked into her office that morning.

The reason behind the no fraternization policy with the Stampede had never been clearer than in the moment she got to Logan's file. Conflict of interest indeed.

It was her job to read the information, but part of her felt like she was betraying him just having the file on her desk.

She stared at it for a full five minutes, chewing on her bottom lip while their conversation from the night of the charity dinner echoed inside her head.

"Not doing your research?"

"On your personal life? No, I prefer it when you tell me things like people do in normal relationships."

And she'd known what she was going to find when she opened that file, too. Known that Madison was going to be in there somewhere. It was information she shouldn't know about in the first place, and there was a guilt associated with this fact she couldn't quite get over.

She'd be lying if she said she didn't want to know everything about Logan. She just wanted *him* to tell her.

And it wasn't like he wasn't sharing other things with her, so she wasn't entirely in the dark about who he was or his past. Hell, she'd spent all of the day before with him, his brother, and sister. They'd grilled steaks and corn on the cob and whiled away the afternoon sitting around his table outside talking.

She was regaled with stories of the three siblings growing up. How they literally did have to walk uphill in the snow to go to school. How their parents had supported all of their dreams, driving Logan to hockey practice at five in the morning, buying Liam a used guitar when he was seven, and setting up a sewing studio in the attic for Adele.

Abby learned that there was a three-year age difference between Logan and Liam, and a seven-year gap between Logan and Adele. She also learned that younger or not, Adele could hold her own against her two older brothers. It had taken Abby about a second to see just how protective all three siblings were for one another, but there was a protectiveness that Liam and Adele had for Logan that went beyond anything Abby had ever seen before.

And she completely got it, too. Because she was finding that she was getting pretty damn protective of him as well. That was what happened when you were in love with someone. That fact still terrified her to a level she wasn't entirely prepared for. But it was a fact nonetheless. A fact that was made even clearer when her computer dinged with an e-mail from Gemma.

She clicked on the file to find a picture of Logan, Jace, and Andre dressed in superhero costumes at the hospital. This was the day that Logan had dressed up as Captain America, half of his face covered up by the blue mask. Jace was Thor wearing a long blond wig and a cape, and Andre was sporting the Iron Man suit.

All three men were standing by the bed of a patient, a little boy no more than eight. The child was kneeling on the bed and smiling as the men posed behind him. Jace was ruffling the boy's short blond hair while the other two men grinned at the camera.

Abby,

I just came across this and remembered talking about it at the charity dinner. Thought you'd want to see the good that your boys are doing.

—Gemma

A knock on the open door had Abby looking up at her assistant.

"You okay?" Brooke asked, tilting her head to the side, her eyes focusing on Abby.

"Yeah," she lied, forcing a smile onto her lips. "Just tired."

"Ready to go to Clementine's for lunch? Maybe a meal will give you a boost. Make you feel beyond better."

"Yeah. I'll be right out." Abby nodded.

She closed the file and stuck it on top of the stack before she turned back to her computer. She glared at the document on her screen before she saved it, thinking she'd just messed with Pandora's box.

She couldn't get over the dread coursing through her as she grabbed her purse and left her office.

* * *

Clementine's was a five-star French soul food restaurant in downtown Jacksonville. It was only a ten-minute walk from the Poseidon Arena, but as the April sun was glaring and the humidity was rising off the concrete in waves, Abby drove. No need to get sweaty and uncomfortable for the rest of the day, especially as she would be working late.

The final game of the season was the following evening, the playoffs were just around the corner, and the Stampede were currently number one in their conference by a fifteen-point lead. A lot of guests of the team were coming to the game. Logan had invited Dale and Virginia Rigels, along with Virginia's boyfriend Marlin Yance, Hamilton, Mel, and Bennett.

Dale was now officially in remission, and Logan had promised him a game whenever that happened. But Logan had done more than that. He'd paid for their rooms at the fanciest hotel in Jacksonville and provided all of their meals.

Count on Logan to go above and beyond.

A new ache bloomed through her chest. It wasn't something she was used to, bittersweet and filled with a deep longing. The more she found out about him, the more he shared with her, the more she knew he was it. And there was a certainty to it that she couldn't deny. Not ever again. That terrified yet thrilled feeling overwhelmed her. It was so beyond complicated.

But he'd said it at the very beginning of this whole thing, during their night spent in Mirabelle: *"Simple is entirely overrated, I'll take complicated any day."*

She was in love with him, there was no doubt. She'd never fallen faster or harder. And she wanted more. She was tired of dealing with the constraints of their secret relationship. It was all or nothing. And she had to figure out how to get it all.

"Are you sure you're okay?" Brooke asked as they got out of the car and Abby gave her keys to the valet. "You're too quiet."

She didn't even have time to answer before they ran into Gemma who was heading out of the restaurant.

"Abby!" the woman exclaimed, grabbing on to Abby's shoulders and bringing her in for a hug, kissing her on the cheek before letting go. "Looks like I get to see you a day early, what a pleasure."

Gemma and Alejandro were coming to the game the following evening, where they would be sitting in the owner's box.

"How was your lunch?" Brooke asked as Gemma gave her an equally warm greeting.

"Didn't even order appetizers before Alejandro got a call for a patient. Life of a doctor. He had to run out so I settled the bill for our drinks."

"Did you eat?" Abby asked.

"No, I don't usually mind eating alone, but I just wasn't feeling it today. Decided I'd pick up a sandwich before I headed back to the office."

"Care to join Brooke and me? The more the merrier."

Gemma beamed as she nodded. "I'd love to."

* * *

As they finished up their meal, Brooke saw a friend of hers from across the restaurant. She excused herself to go say hi, leaving Gemma and Abby.

"Thank you for the picture," Abby said as she took a sip of her pomegranate sweet tea.

"It was no problem." Gemma smiled. "Mr. James and his friends have been a joy to have at the hospital. They are very good men."

"Yes." Abby nodded. "They are."

"Maybe one of them more than the others?" Gemma leaned back in her chair as she gave Abby a significant look.

"I…" Abby's mind froze. How could she possibly know?

"He is special, Mr. James. It is hard to find a man like that in this day and age. A man who looks at a woman from across a crowded room and his adoration is apparent to those who know the look of a man who is in love. And the look of a woman who loves him right back."

The blood rushed from Abby's head.

Did Logan look at her that way? Like a man in love?

"No need to worry." Gemma reached across the table and patted Abby's hand. "Your secret is safe with me. But I would imagine this secret is getting to be a bit of a hassle."

"To say the least."

"Maybe there is a way we can all get what we want."

"And how's that?" Hope filled Abby's stomach as she looked across the table at Gemma, the woman who might be the answer to a very complicated problem.

"I want you to work for me, Abby. I've wanted it since the moment I met you. You're smart, persistent, and strong. Your determination would be a massive asset to my public relations department. A department that I want you to run. St. Ignatius is growing, and our cancer center is going to be the top facility in the south. Your talent is out of this world, and in my humble opinion, you will not reach it in an office of colleagues who drastically underestimate you. You are a star, Abby, and you will shine wherever you are, but I think that you will shine much brighter with us."

Abby sat in stunned silence. She knew she was good at her job. Knew exactly what she was capable of, but never had she been called a star.

The waiter came with the bill, and before Abby was able to have her body connect with her brain to grab it, Gemma snatched it off the table.

"No." Abby shook her head, somehow managing to get her tongue unstuck from the roof of her mouth. "We asked you to join us."

"Yes, but I just offered you a job. So this is a business lunch. My treat."

Brooke was making her way back to them from across the room, a smile on her face.

"And the offer extends to your assistant, too. I think Brooke's potential is something that should be cultivated as well. You think on it, Abby. I know you most likely wouldn't be able to leave until the playoffs are over, hopefully with the Stanley Cup in the hands of the Stampede. But I'd like an answer sooner than later."

The waiter and Brooke made it back to the table at the same time. Gemma put her credit card back into her pocketbook and signed the piece of paper before they stood and headed out the door.

They made small talk as the valets went to retrieve the two cars, Abby's mind spinning the entire time.

"It was lovely seeing you ladies," Gemma said as she kissed both women on the cheek in turn. "If there are any developments with anything, you know where to reach me." She smiled at both of them as she slipped her sunglasses onto her nose and got into her car.

Brooke went through the schedule for the rest of the week as they drove back to the office. It gave Abby something to focus on besides that illuminating conversation at lunch. And it worked right up until she walked into her office.

Rodger Dingle came striding out. He stopped short when he saw her, like a kid caught with his hand in the cookie jar.

"What were you doing in my office?"

"Something to hide, D.C.?"

"No." She shook her head. "But as it's my office I'd appreciate it if you weren't in it when I wasn't."

"Well, isn't that nice? There are a lot of things I'd appreciate. Like tomorrow's updated itinerary, which I had to forward to myself." He held up his phone.

"I sent it this morning, Mr. Dingle." Brooke smiled sweetly as she dropped her purse on her desk.

"Maybe it got lost in translation, so I got it myself. I'll leave you two to get some work done."

Abby didn't say anything as he turned and walked out the door. There was no point. And as she stared at his retreating back, Gemma's words echoed in her head.

"Your talent is out of this world, and in my humble opinion, you will not reach it in an office of colleagues who drastically underestimate you."

Underestimated and undermined.

Leaving the Stampede was looking better and better. She'd be able to run her own department and not have to deal with anyone like Dingle. *And* she and Logan wouldn't have to keep quiet about their relationship.

Logan.

When she walked back into her office her eyes landed on the stack of files. She grabbed his and pulled out everything that had to do with Madison. She stuck them in the shredder before she opened the document on her computer, hitting the Delete button.

She was wrong. There was no conflict of interest. She chose Logan.

Chapter 13

Truths Untold

The Poseidon Arena was packed with waves of people wearing black and gray for the Stampede. There were little spots of red, white, and blue for the New York Rangers, but their fans were vastly outnumbered tonight.

Abby made her way through the crowd and toward the front doors. Logan had hired a car from the hotel for Dale and the rest of his entourage. Abby was actually joining the group for the game, so she took on the responsibility of meeting them outside and escorting them to their seats.

The line of cars at drop-off was long, but Abby's timing was perfect. She spotted Mel's curly head emerging from a limo, Bennett standing next to the door as he held his hand out for her to grab. Virginia Rigels was already standing on the pavement, hand in hand with a tall man in his late fifties. He had thin graying hair and was wearing cowboy boots with his jeans and a black Stampede jersey.

A second later Dale was getting out of the limo. He looked less frail than he had in February, more color in his cheeks and a short layer of dark brown hair on the top of his head.

The last out of the limo was Hamilton, who spotted Abby immediately.

She smiled as she headed over to the group, giving them all hugs in turn and getting introduced to Marlin, the only person she hadn't met before.

"He was visiting his daughter when we had the birthday party. She'd just had a baby, Marlin's first granddaughter," Virginia explained as they all made their way into the arena.

"Well, I'm glad you could make it out for this, Marlin. You all get settled in to the hotel okay?" she asked.

"Yeah we did," Dale answered enthusiastically. "I think our room is bigger than my mom's house. It's freaking massive."

"Logan booked two deluxe suites." Virginia shook her head like it was all too much. "Really, it wasn't necessary, especially with everything else he's done."

"Oh, the tickets are nothing really." Abby waved off Virginia's words. "All of the players get them, and he wanted you all to come as his guests tonight."

Virginia's head tilted to the side, her eyes going soft. "I wasn't talking about the tickets. I will never be able to repay that man for what he's done for Dale. What he's done for me."

"Wh—" Abby was just about to get the question out when Dale grabbed on to his mother's arm as the rink came into view. The Zamboni was making its way around the edge.

"It would be the icing on the cake if I could take a ride on that." He grinned.

"Yeah, I think you've about reached the max on awesome," Hamilton said as he looked around the arena.

Abby's phone buzzed and she grabbed on to the rail as they headed down the stairs. She looked down at the screen to see a text from Logan.

You with Dale and Hamilton?

Yes, she typed out as she paused at the end of their aisle while everyone found their seats.

Bring them down.

Abby grinned as she looked up. "I think you were wrong on reaching the max of awesome, Hamilton. You and Dale want to go to the locker rooms?"

Both of them were out of their seats in under a second.

* * *

Logan had asked Coach Bale if Dale and Hamilton could come down and meet the team. Bale was all about focus before a game; he was a no-nonsense kind of guy and didn't want his players distracted by anything or anyone.

But once Logan explained the situation and the fact that he'd developed a relationship with them, Bale had agreed.

"Five minutes. That's it. They can shake some hands. Get some autographs and then back to their seats. Got it?"

"Got it."

But it wasn't just the players who were talking to Dale and Hamilton now. Bale was laughing, actually laughing, as he signed one of the hats being passed around the room and talked to a beaming Dale.

The kid's teeth could be seen from every single direction his smile was so wide. And he wasn't the only one smiling, either. Abby was standing by the doors grinning as she watched the two boys float around the room like they were on cloud nine.

Thank you, she mouthed.

He just shrugged his shoulders. It was no skin off his nose and it would be a story those kids would tell for years to come.

His eyes might've lingered on Abby for a moment longer than they should have, but who could blame him? She was wearing strappy black heels and a gray dress that he had every intention of depositing on his bedroom floor tonight.

They'd spent the previous night apart—she stayed at work late and he had to get up early for training and practice. He'd missed her and he had every intention of making up for lost time.

Abby was the one who pulled her gaze away first as the door next to her opened and Dumbass from the PR department walked through it. The smile on her face disappeared and her back went up instantly. She was clearly uncomfortable around this guy, and it took everything in Logan to stop himself from walking across the room and going to her.

But Abby was the one moving away toward Dale and Hamilton. Their five minutes was up and the team needed to get ready for the game. Logan headed in that direction as well, wanting to get a quick word with the boys before they left.

"Thank you so much for letting them come down here," Abby said to Coach Bale.

"Something like this? Not a problem. You boys better come to more games, got it?"

"Yes, sir," Dale and Hamilton said in unison.

Abby turned to look at Logan and he gestured to the door. "I'll walk you out."

She nodded before she led the way, Dale and Hamilton in between them. When they stepped out into the hallway, Dale turned to Logan and stuck out his hand. The kid had a firm grip and he looked Logan straight in the eye when he spoke.

"I really can't thank you enough for what you've done for me."

"You deserved something fun."

"I'm not talking about tonight." Dale shook his head as he let go of Logan's hand. "I'm talking about the fact that you paid for my hospital bills."

Logan stilled as he shook the kid's hand. No one knew about that. He could feel Abby's stare boring into the side of his head, and he saw her jaw drop from the corner of his eye.

He had no idea what to say. He couldn't lie. Couldn't tell the kid that it hadn't been him. It just didn't feel right.

"Look, I know the donation was anonymous. But as it happened about a week after I met you, and there aren't any other millionaires that I've met, I figured it was you. You were my hero long before you came to visit me two months ago. And it had everything to do with your mad skills on the ice."

Logan laughed.

"But now? Now you're the man who is keeping my mother from working herself into an early grave. Something that she would've had to do to keep *me* out of an early grave. You've given us both a gift. And I want you to know that I'm going to pay it forward. One day, I'm going to give it back to someone else just because it's the right thing."

"You sure you're only seventeen?" Logan asked, beyond impressed with the kid.

"Pretty sure." He nodded.

Logan held his hand out for another handshake, but when Dale put his hand in Logan's, Logan pulled the kid in for a hug. When they broke apart, Dale had to reach up and wipe his eyes, and Logan felt his throat constrict just a little bit.

"You ever need anything, you call me, okay?"

Dale nodded again.

"And like Coach Bale said, you better come to more games."

"We'll be there." Dale grinned.

"I'll see you later, Hamilton." Logan shook the hand of the other kid before he turned back to the locker room.

He caught Abby's gaze, saw the shock and awe in her eyes, and the tears that trailed down her cheeks.

"Don't look at me like that, Red," he said just low enough for her to hear.

"I can't help it." She glanced down the hallway, empty besides Dale and Hamilton, before she turned back to him and grabbed the front of his jersey. "You're a good man, Logan James," she said right before she pressed her lips to his.

Her tongue dipped into his mouth and he opened wide, letting her inside in all of her splendid glory. But it was over pretty much the second it had started. She let go of his jersey and pulled back.

She straightened her dress before she turned back to the wide-eyed boys and pointed her finger between the two of them. "You didn't see that."

"See what?" Hamilton asked, cracking a smile.

"I think I just went temporarily blind," Dale said as he shrugged.

She moved toward the kids, putting her hands on their shoulders as she led them away. Both boys were already taller than her. Hamilton probably just under six feet, and Dale not that far behind.

Abby looked over her shoulder at Logan just before they rounded the corner, giving him a smile she reserved just for him. He couldn't help mirroring it as he turned and headed back to the locker room.

He'd chosen to ignore the conversation he'd had with Liam on Sunday. Had told himself he wasn't going to worry about it.

Was sticking to his guns that it was too soon to have fallen for Abby.

The thing was, he was only deluding himself.

He had fallen in love with her. Had fallen in love with her two months ago, in a cabin in Tennessee, on Valentine's Day.

* * *

To say that the game was intense would be an understatement. Abby was on the edge of her seat all night as the score bounced back and forth. In the beginning of the third period, the Rangers pulled ahead by two, but then Logan managed to do something remarkable.

He'd gotten a hat trick rounding out the Stampede's score to an even six over the Rangers five. He scored that last goal with nineteen seconds left on the clock, and the roar from the crowd had been deafening.

She watched the team skate around the rink, watched as Logan pulled off his helmet, his eyes scanning the crowd and landing on her.

He'd been the final factor in her decision tonight. He'd been the reason she'd gone up to the president's box during the first intermission and told Gemma she'd be accepting the job at St. Ignatius. He'd been the reason more than anything else.

She was done hiding their relationship. Done keeping one of the best things that had ever happened to her a secret.

He'd frustrated her so much when she first met him. She'd thought he was difficult, and moody, and uncaring.

But she'd been wrong. So damn wrong.

Well, she'd been mostly wrong. He could be difficult, complicated as he liked to say. And there were those moments when he could be moody. But he wasn't uncaring. No, he was the kindest man she knew. Compassionate beyond words.

She still couldn't believe he'd paid for Dale's medical bills. There were very few people in this world who would do that for someone who was practically a stranger. But Logan had. He'd done it selflessly. People were shaped by their pain, Abby knew that good and well, but he'd done something remarkable with it.

Since Abby was ten years old she'd been terrified of giving her heart to a man, and she'd done a pretty good job of keeping it guarded. Until Logan James came into the picture. After that first night they spent together, she never had a chance.

Who was she kidding? She'd been fighting a losing battle from the moment she met him. But if she was going to give her heart to anyone, there was no one better than this man.

She was all in. The certainty of her decision was staggering and she was more than a little dazed as she said goodbye to everyone and headed down to the pressroom at the arena. A couple of players had been requested for interviews for the post-game wrap-up, Logan being one of them.

When Abby walked into the room she spotted Dingle in the corner talking to Howard Lewis. Lewis was a reporter who was known for not having a soul. He was the one who wrote the article about Logan and Proctor getting into a fight in the locker room, the one who knew way more of the story than anyone outside of the Stampede should.

She watched as the two men shook hands, and an uneasiness tightened her stomach.

But before Abby could say or do anything—though really what the hell was she going to do?—Coach Bale, Logan, Jace, Andre, and Proctor filed into the room. All the players sported wet hair from their recent showers, and they all wore button-up shirts in varying shades of gray, and black blazers.

The room filled with flashes as the men all took their seats behind a long table. Logan and Andre on Coach Bales's left, Jace and Proctor on the right.

Abby looked over toward Dingle, who was making his way to the back of the room. The look of excited glee in his eyes made the back of her neck prickle.

* * *

Logan normally didn't mind press conferences. He would sit there and answer as many questions about the game as the reporters threw at him, no problem. But tonight he was eager to go home, eager to celebrate tonight's victory with Abby.

"I have a question for Mr. James," one of the reporters said as he focused on Logan. "You've been playing hockey in the majors for seven years now. The last four years, this year in particular, have definitely surpassed your career in the beginning. What's different now?"

"You're only as good as the team you're on. Jace, Andre, and I have learned to anticipate each other's moves. I'd say it has way more to do with us figuring each other out. Our line just clicked and you're seeing the results of that."

"So you work better with them more than other players?" another reporter asked. "For example, Kent Proctor. It's no secret you two had an altercation earlier this season. Does your off the ice relationship affect you on the ice?"

"Our *off the ice relationship*? You make it sound like we're going to prom or something."

The room filled with low chuckles.

"Kent and I are colleagues. We mesh just fine on and off the ice." At least Logan thought so. They dealt with each other when they were playing and ignored each other the rest of the time.

"And what about your other off the ice endeavors?" a voice called out among the flashes.

Logan looked to the left and spotted Howard Lewis, a prime example of why he tended to dislike the media.

"It's no secret that I like to keep my personal life private," Logan said. "So my off the ice endeavors aren't up for discussion."

"What about when you bring your personal life into the public? There were two kids in the locker room tonight before the game started, *your* personal guests for the evening."

"We had a few minutes before the game started, and I invited them down. It's not unheard of. And a lot of the guys had guests at the game tonight."

"Yeah, but one of your guests is a kid who's in remission from cancer. You visited him in his hometown a couple of months ago and you paid his hospital bills. That's a pretty generous thing, don't you think? Remarkable even."

The only sound that could be heard was the constant click and flash from the cameras.

How the fuck did he know?

"I don't know where you're going with this, Howard," Logan said.

"You're visiting the cancer ward at St. Ignatius and bringing other players." He indicated Andre and Jace with the end of his pen. "Dressing up as superheroes and such is a pretty exceptional thing. And I was just wondering if you were going to go further with this new endeavor of yours?"

Okay, so this was a story that he knew wasn't going to stay secret for long. It was only a matter of time before someone found out, but Logan knew by the look in the guy's eyes that this wasn't where the story was about to end.

"I haven't thought that far out." Logan shook his head slowly, a foreboding in his stomach.

"Well, you're becoming an example, Mr. James, and for much more than your athleticism. I'm sure your fans would be fascinated to know where this motivation came from. Is this a new mission that has to do with your daughter who died from the disease eight years ago?"

The room filled with an incessant chatter, questions indiscernible among the masses, but Logan could barely hear it above the buzzing in his ears.

This wasn't happening.

Was. Not. Happening.

Madison was off limits more than anything else in his life. She wasn't anybody's business. She wasn't a spectacle, someone to be pitied. No, none of that.

She was his daughter. Not a story.

The walls around him began to narrow, started closing in on him. He had to get the fuck out of here.

He wasn't even aware that he'd stood up, and he was pretty sure that the force guiding him out of the room was something beyond him. Because every other instinct told him to turn around and knock the shit out of Howard Lewis.

* * *

The need to get Logan alone and talk to him was overwhelming, but that wasn't going to happen. There were seven people currently crowded in the office Abby was standing in: Adam Lindbergh (the head of the PR department and Abby's boss),

Coach Bale, Rodger Dingle, Dominic Ferguson (Logan's agent), and Brooke who couldn't tear her eyes away from the TV mounted on the wall.

A series of images flickered, first the clip of Logan walking out of the press conference. Next flashed a couple pictures of Dale and Hamilton in the locker room, talking to the players as they got their hats signed. Then the one of Madison that had been attached to her obituary.

Abby was battling between panic mode and crisis mode. She was the reason this was all happening...well, part of it anyways.

Rodger Dingle was the real reason.

The puzzle pieces were all falling into place, Dingle coming out of her office the day before. She hadn't logged out of her computer, hadn't locked her office. There had never been a need for it. Why would she be concerned that another person in the PR department might go through her things and leak information about the team they both worked for?

She'd made it so easy for him, too. Those files had been right there on her desk, Logan's on top. And then all of her e-mails had been right there for him to pull up as well. The e-mail with the picture of him at the hospital that was now flashing across the screen.

"I want to know how the *hell* he found out about all of this." Logan's jaw ticked as he pointed to the screen.

"I'm sure the kids tweeted those pictures. Posted them on Facebook or whatever," Dingle said.

"I don't think so." Abby shook her head. "Neither of those boys are on Twitter and their Facebook pages are private."

"How do you know?" Dingle asked, his skepticism clear as he looked at her.

"Because I talked to both of them after this happened."

"It just takes one person who is friends with either of them to share it. Then it's all over the Internet," Lindbergh said. His round face had taken on a red hue and he kept running his hand across his bald head.

"I know that, but Howard Lewis knew a lot of information, much more than can be found on Facebook. Logan visited Dale months ago, and it's just coming out now. Just coming out today, along with everything else." Abby's eyes narrowed as she turned to look at the man who she *knew* was responsible for the leak.

"I don't understand why we weren't sharing this information in the first place," Dingle said. "It's great press."

"He's a kid recovering from cancer. His disease isn't something for us to use for good press," Logan ground out through his teeth. "He wants to share it, he can. It isn't something for us to exploit."

"But you did take the opportunity to exploit it. Didn't you, Rodger?" Abby asked. "I saw you talking to Howard before the conference, maybe you know how he got that information."

"You're accusing me of doing this, D.C.? Telling secrets? Selling out our players? I think if anyone's moral integrity for this job needs to be looked at, it should be yours. You know James here on a much more *intimate* level than I do." He took a step closer to her, the malevolence in his eyes clear. "Now I know the secret to your success. You screw your clients. But I get it, you have to be on the bottom to get to the top."

Abby reeled back like she'd been slapped.

Logan moved from his corner of the room, the rage radiating off of him as he stepped between her and Dingle and got right up in the other guy's face. "I'd be careful with what you say about Abby, Dilbert."

"It's Dingle," Rodger said as he puffed out his chest.

"I don't *fucking* care."

"Logan." Abby reached out, her fingers wrapping around his forearm as she gently pulled. "Stop."

He came with little resistance, let himself be led away. And really Abby needed to put as much distance between the two of them as possible, because if she could prove that it was Dingle behind this, there was no telling what would happen.

"You see?" Dingle said as he turned to Lindbergh. "You see?" He waved his hands frantically at Logan and Abby. "This is what I'm talking about. If anyone was able to get insider information on James it was D.C. over here."

"Abby, is this true?" Lindbergh asked, turning to look at her. "Do you and James have something beyond a professional relationship?"

There was no more denying it. "Yes." She nodded.

"I see." Lindbergh's head knocked back just slightly on his neck, and his eyebrows rose up his forehead. "Did this start before or after the altercation in the locker room between James and Proctor?"

"Before."

"Well, this complicates matters." Lindbergh shook his head.

"All of the problems started to happen when she showed up," Dingle said, shaking his head, acting justified in his disapproval. "The whole situation with Kilpatrick getting caught at that private club with that singer." He ticked off one finger on his hand. "The altercation in the locker room." He ticked off a second finger. "*This*." He ticked off a third finger. "Do you get your contacts at the hospital to spy on him or something? Get Gemma Faro to send you pictures of him in those ridiculous superhero costumes?" He gestured to the TV as the picture he was talking about came up on the screen.

And there it was.

"How did you know that, Rodger? How did you know Gemma sent me that picture?" Abby asked.

"I…" Dingle froze, his hand still in mid-air, his mouth hanging open.

"Something else that should be noted," Brooke said, walking close to the TV that she hadn't pulled her gaze from once. "Neither Dale nor Hamilton took this picture. Look," she said, pointing, "they both have their phones in their hands. You can clearly see them." She turned and looked at Abby, sweeping her long blonde hair off her shoulder. "Who else was in the locker room?"

"Besides the players and me?" Coach Bale asked. "Just Ms. Fields and him," he said, pointing to Dingle.

"And D.C. must have taken the picture," Dingle said, apparently recovering from his inability to answer earlier.

"No." Brooke shook her head. "When the picture filters through again you can see Abby standing off to the side. It's only the side of her, but as the person in the picture is shorter than six feet and wearing a dress and heels, I'm guessing it's her."

"Rodger is the one who is behind all of this," Abby said, turning to Lindbergh. "And I'm pretty sure he targeted Logan because he doesn't like me."

There was a move behind her and she turned just in time to see Bale and Ferguson restraining Logan.

"You did this?" His voice was low, shaking with rage as he glared at Dingle.

"Yes, he did." She nodded, talking to everyone in the room. "Rodger must've overheard Dale talking to Logan outside the locker room right before the game. And yesterday I caught him coming out of my office, where I'm almost positive he got the picture Gemma sent of the guys at the hospital and the information about Logan's daughter."

"*What?*" The word came out on a growl and Abby looked at Logan. His eyes were narrowed on her in disbelief.

"Logan." She held out her hands as she took a step forward, but he backed away, before he pulled out of the grip of the two men who were still attempting to restrain him.

"Why was there information about Madison in your office?"

Abby's hands fell away in the space between them. She took a deep breath as she looked at him, words suddenly failing *her*.

"Why, Abby?" He repeated his question, a hardness in his eyes that made her stomach hurt.

"I did background checks on all the players. It wasn't just you, and your—"

"Stop." He held up his hands, silencing her. "I don't need to hear any more." He shook his head as he took another step back from her. "Somebody better fucking fix this," he said to the room at large before he turned and walked through the door.

Abby followed on instinct, ignoring the calls of her name behind her. She didn't care who she was walking away from. All she cared about was who had just walked away from her.

She had to run down the hallway to talk to him, her heels slowing her down too much to catch up to Logan's long strides. There was no use for it; she stopped and placed her palm flat on the wall as she leaned against it, unzipping the back of her shoe and dropping it to the floor. She shifted to stand on her other foot a moment later, the other shoe hitting the ground with a thud before she started running to catch him.

"Logan, please." She grabbed his arm just before he reached the elevator doors. "Let me explain."

He turned to her and shook his head, pulling his arm from

her grasp. "I don't care." He reached for the button by the elevator and pounded it with his fist.

"You don't understand," she pleaded.

"No, *you* don't understand." He turned to look at her, a look of loathing in his eyes. "Being with you was a mistake from the beginning."

For the second time that evening, she flinched back like she'd been slapped.

"You were right, when you said this was too complicated. It's a conflict of interest to be with you. It's like you said, I despise what you do with almost every fiber of my being. This story about Madison? It's out there because of you."

"I…" She swallowed hard, her throat not really wanting to cooperate. "I'm sorry." She didn't know what else to say. The words he'd just spoken felt like a physical blow.

"I don't care."

The elevator dinged behind them, the doors sliding open. He took a step back from her and got on, shaking his head in cold disgust.

The doors slid shut and just like that, Logan was gone.

For so long she'd told herself all or nothing when it came to him. It was clear she was getting nothing.

Chapter 14

Maybe I'll Get Over You ...
or Maybe Not

Logan stared out at the darkness behind his backyard. A few lights flickered off his pool and the steady sound of the Intracoastal Waterway filled the night air along with the cicadas. He leaned back, the rocking chair creaking against the floorboards of the porch.

He finished off his beer, the third of the night, and waited for the buzz in his head to drown out the boos from earlier that evening.

They'd lost their first game of the playoffs, spectacularly so, the Boston Bruins scoring five while they enjoyed a big fat goose egg.

"Want another?" Jace said from the rocker next to him, popping the cap on a bottle and handing it to Logan before he even had a chance to answer.

He took the bottle and tipped it back, the cold beer filling his mouth and washing down his throat, bringing him closer to that buzz he was chasing.

He'd left the stadium as soon as he showered and changed,

dodging the cameras that had been following him the last couple of days and wanting nothing but to be alone. But he didn't get that wish.

Jace had shown up at the house about twenty minutes after Logan arrived home, two six-packs of beer in hand. They'd been sitting outside for the last hour, and in between the lulls of silence, they talked about the disaster of a game they'd just played.

Because reliving things was apparently the best policy these days.

It had been three days since Madison had become news. Three days since Logan was added to the continuing cycle of stories that filtered through every sports program broadcasted. Three days since he'd walked out on Abby.

Whenever he thought about her, the pain was staggering. But it came twofold, one from missing her, and the other from what she'd caused to be shared with the world.

Rodger Dingle might be the real reason everything had come to light, but no matter how Logan looked at it, Abby was partially to blame.

It was more than a bit ironic that the Stampede PR department was creating chaos PR for the Stampede. Both Dingle and Abby had been fired, Dingle for his sabotage and Abby for her relationship with Logan. None of this had remained a secret, either.

Dingle had sold everybody out, telling his side of the story to anyone who would listen. Turns out a lot of people wanted to listen, wanted to know the whole story. That's why they were harassing Logan.

It was just too bad he wasn't talking.

"So do you want to discuss that steal from Gordon in the second period? How you couldn't score to save your life? Or would you like to discuss the real reason you epically sucked out on that ice tonight?"

Logan brought the bottle to his mouth again and took a swig while he held up his middle finger with his other hand.

Jace laughed as he opened another bottle for himself. "You know I'm not saying you're the reason we lost tonight. Not at all. Every single guy on that ice sucked something fierce. We've done so well this season that we've become cocky arrogant bastards. But there was something going on with you tonight that went above and beyond that."

"Huh, I wonder what that is?"

"So, you're just going to walk away from this? One bump in the road and you're done?"

Logan stopped rocking and turned to look at Jace. "*One* bump. Are you fucking kidding me?"

"You think she wanted any of this to happen? Do you seriously think that Abby wanted Madison's death to be all over kingdom come? That she wanted to hurt you? Are *you* fucking kidding *me*? I really thought you were smarter than that, thought that you were figuring things out as you were letting her into your life. Something that's shocked the hell out of me these last couple of months, because I was beginning to think that wasn't possible."

"What the hell is that supposed to mean?"

"What do you think it means, Logan? I haven't seen you with her all that much, but I've seen you. And you're different. Happy even, which is something I haven't seen all that often in the four years we've been friends. And another thing, in all that time you've mentioned Madison once, and that was when you were drunk off your ass. You don't typically let new people in. I still don't understand how I got past the barrier."

"Sheer force of will probably."

A grin cracked Jace's lips as he brought the bottle to his mouth and took a drink. He swallowed as he studied Logan, then cleared his throat before he spoke. "I consider you to be my best friend, both on the team and off. Since I've known you, being with Abby is the happiest that I've ever seen you. And right now, right in this moment, you are the most miserable bastard I've ever met, and that's saying something considering who my father is."

Logan turned away and looked out at the backyard again, the truth in Jace's words too much to deal with while he was looking at the guy.

"Now I know that you don't agree with it, but she was just doing her job," Jace said conversationally, the squeak of his chair picking up as he began to rock.

"It's a shitty job." The darkness seemed to intensify around them. Logan's fingers clutched the sweating bottle of beer, the coldness of the glass leaching into his hand.

"I get that Madison is not and was not a small part of your life, Logan. She was your daughter, and her death sucked you into this massive black hole." Jace's voice was no longer conversational but dead serious. "But you need to pull your head out of your ass."

Logan's head jerked as he turned to look at his friend. "You've got about two seconds."

"Or what? What are you going to do? Actually no." He shook his head. "I'm going to tell you what you're going to do. You're going to listen to what I've got to say, Logan. Because when Abby came along, she brought you out of this black hole that you've been living in. That you've *barely* been surviving in. And she risked a lot to be with you. Risked her career, her reputation, and her heart I'm guessing because for whatever reason I'm pretty sure she fell in love with your stubborn ass. And you want to blame her for the truth about Madison getting out."

"You don't get it." Logan was barely able to get the words out. "I miss her every damn day."

"I know that you miss her. And I don't fully understand that grief. The pain of burying a child is something no parent should ever have to know. So tell me, do you really think Abby was going to do something with that information? Do you really think she would try to hurt you like that? Now even I'm a smarter man than to think that." Jace took another sip of his beer and swallowed.

"Thinking and knowing are two different things."

"Yeah, but what does it feel like? You know the truth. You know it by how it feels. And the truth here is that you fell in love and it terrifies the shit out of you. So you think she's done something to disappoint you, and at the first opportunity you're running because it's the only way you know how to deal."

"Seriously? You want to lecture *me* about coping mechanisms?" Logan asked.

"Hey." Jace held up his hands in defense, one palm flat out, the other still wrapped around his beer. "I never said I was the poster child for dealing with my baggage in a healthy way."

Logan snorted. "No kidding."

Yeah, Jace "dealt" with his issues by going on benders of meaningless sex. Logan knew that route good and well. It didn't work. Especially when you found the person that makes it meaningful.

And losing that person? Yeah, it sucked all the more.

"I'm also not the guy who's walking away from something because he's scared of getting hurt again." Jace shook his head. "And it's like I said before, you don't typically let new people in. But you let Abby in, faster than anything I've ever seen. She took down your defenses, and that's why you're so angry. All of this other stuff that you're blaming her for? That wasn't on her, man.

That was on a guy who it looks like was hell bent on sabotaging her and you. And from where I'm sitting? He's winning and you're losing. And you're losing something much bigger than a game or a trophy."

And there was that staggering pain again. The pain that came from losing Abby, from missing her. Yeah it had only been three days, and yeah he'd gone longer than this without seeing her, without talking to her. But there hadn't been a finality to it.

There hadn't been that possibility that it was all over. That he'd kissed her for the last time. That he'd never make love to her again. That he'd never hear her laugh, feel her up against him, dance with her, or see her bare feet sticking out from the bottom of the comforter while she slept soundly in his bed.

Was he ready to walk away from all of that? To walk away from her?

* * *

Never in his life did Logan think he'd be voluntarily walking into the Stampede PR department. He'd pretty much vowed to have nothing to do with them ever again after the most recent clusterfuck of events. But circumstances being what they were, he was here.

He'd gone to Abby's that morning before practice, the need to talk to her stronger than he'd been prepared for. He didn't even realize he'd been driving in that direction. But when he pulled up in front of her condo she wasn't there, her car glaringly absent from the driveway.

He hadn't called. He didn't know what he would say. He needed to see her for the right words to come. Talking into a machine? Yeah, that just wasn't going to cut it.

It had been a miracle that he'd somehow managed to pull it together for practice, but a guy only needed his ass handed to him once in a twenty-four-hour period.

Then after practice, he had a repeat performance of going in a direction before he'd consciously made the decision. As he walked through those glass doors and into the room, the back of his neck started to itch, and he'd be surprised if he hadn't just broken out in a rash.

He made his way down to the end of the hall, where Abby's office had been, in search of Brooke. But when he got to the small reception area, he found boxes stacked all along Brooke's desk and her walls were free from the framed art that had been there before.

He stuck his head into the open door that had been Abby's office. Besides the computer monitor on the desk and the office furniture, it was cleared out. The built-in bookcases behind the desk were bare, all of her books and pictures gone. Her diplomas were missing from the wall, the deep blue rug no longer spread out in the middle of the floor, and the plant she'd kept in the corner had disappeared.

The arena was visible through the open blinds on the windows. The light from the sun broken by the thin plastic rectangles caused lines to form on the walls and floor of her very empty office.

It was just...sad. Sad without her. Well, he could relate to that now, couldn't he?

"Can I help you?"

Logan turned around to find Brooke. She was wearing jeans and a green polo shirt, her hair pulled back into a high ponytail.

"Logan," she said in surprise. "I didn't expect to see you here."

"Yeah, me either. You leaving?" he asked, indicating the boxes.

He didn't know Brooke all that well, but Abby had talked about her assistant all the time. He hoped she hadn't been fired, too.

"Yes, I resigned with Abby."

"You what? I thought Abby was fired."

"Depends on how you want to look at it I guess." She shrugged. "She accepted another job about two hours before everything went down the other night. So, can you really be fired when you've already resigned?"

"What job did she take?"

"Running the PR department at St. Ignatius. Gemma Faro offered it to her."

"She was leaving the Stampede? Why?" he asked as he folded his arms across his chest and leaned against the doorjamb.

"You don't know?" Brooke raised her eyebrows as she tilted her head to the side and looked at Logan. "Abby didn't tell you?"

"She didn't tell me a lot of things apparently." The words came out a little more bitter than expected.

"You know, she took the job so she could be with you."

"What?" His arms fell to his side and he straightened.

"Well, at least that was part of the reason. I'm going to guess a fifty-one to forty-nine percent split, that extra two going to you. When she asked me to come with her, she told me why she was leaving, full disclosure and all. I mean she's excited about the new job no doubt, but I'm pretty sure she was way more excited about the fact that she didn't have to keep your relationship a secret. A secret that neither of you hid all that well from me, by the way. Well, she was a little bit better than you were, because holy hell when you looked at her it was beyond obvious. But that was just my observation, so—"

"Brooke," he said firmly as he took a step toward her, "where is she?"

Chapter 15

All or Nothing

Abby looked in the rearview mirror as she switched lanes to take the exit that would lead her to her condo. Black streaks trailed down her cheeks and to her jaw. She didn't even want to know the state around her eyes. She could only imagine what the area covered by her sunglasses looked like.

So wearing mascara was officially never going to happen again... not for a while at least. A year, maybe two. That's when she'd be able to function like a normal human being again.

Yeah, *fucking* right.

She wasn't sure why she'd even bothered with makeup this morning. Maybe because it was just part of the routine. Something to do to distract her from the numbing pain. But distractions were few and far between. Hadn't really existed at all since those elevator doors closed and Logan was gone.

Abby had driven to Mirabelle the morning after everything happened; she'd had to get out of town. There'd been absolutely no point for her to stick around, especially after Lindbergh told her she was fired.

"There's nothing I can do." He'd shaken his head, regret clear in his eyes. "You're better than half the department put together, but it's in your contract, Abby."

And what did a couple of months matter anyway? She'd already verbally accepted the job with St. Ignatius and, more important, there was no way in hell she could possibly work for the Stampede when she couldn't have Logan.

All or nothing.

Non-stop tears or not, she wasn't ready to give up on the *all* yet. That much had been made clear to her from some very wise words, from a very wise friend.

"You giving up?" Paige had asked that morning. They'd been sitting on the bed in the guest room, their backs resting on the headboard and their legs stretched out underneath the quilt.

"What else am I supposed to do?" Abby asked as she traced her finger around the rim of her coffee mug. "Because I don't know. He walked out, Paige. Didn't give me a chance to explain anything, to tell him that I chose him, before *he* decided it was over and he...he...just left."

Left *her*.

It was nineteen years ago all over again and the pain was debilitating.

"He's not your father, Abby. This isn't the same thing."

Paige knew exactly where Abby's thoughts had drifted. Best friends had superpowers sometimes. If only they could fix broken hearts, too.

"You sure about that?" Abby asked. "Because it feels pretty damn similar. Neither of them looked back. Neither of them cared. Neither of them fought for me."

Logan had just given up on her. On them.

"Maybe you need to fight."

Abby's finger faltered on the rim of her mug and she looked over at Paige, raising her eyebrows. "Fight for what?"

"Fight for the last cup of coffee," Paige said, holding up her mug. "Fight for the covers at night. Fight for who gets to wash the other's back. Fight for who gets to wash the other's front." She grinned and waggled her eyebrows. "Fight for who gets to pick the song when you dance around the living room. Fight to not fall asleep for just one more second so you can feel his breath on your cheek. Fight for who gets to kiss the other first in the morning. Fight for the moments you get to spend with just each other, the outside world gone. Fight for the moments that you want with him. All of them. Fight for him, Abby."

"What if I can't?"

"What if *you* can't? Okay, who are you and what the hell have you done with Abby Fields?"

The laugh that burst from Abby's mouth quickly turned to a sob. The cup disappeared from her grasp a second later, and she was pulled into Paige's arms where she let the tears loose for about the thirty-ninth time.

"I love him," Abby whispered when she managed to get her breathing under control. It was the first time she'd said it out loud and it was painful to her own ears.

"So go get him."

And that was exactly what Abby was going to do, just as soon as she went home and figured out her next move. Three hours in the car hadn't revealed that.

Nope. She had nothing.

She'd gone over what she was going to say to him. Apologizing. Explaining herself. Anything that it took to get him back.

The problem was she had no idea where he was. She was no longer privy to his schedule. She at least knew that he should be in town because the second game against the Bruins was the following night.

His house was a distinct possibility, and she would head over there just as soon as she got ahold of herself.

Whenever the hell that was.

It was a little after five o'clock when she parked her car in her driveway and turned off the ignition. She flipped the visor down immediately and lifted up her glasses, pushing them back into her hair.

Fantastic. She was a freaking raccoon. Proof positive that waterproof mascara was a good idea. Though she had some doubts as to whether that would've held up. She wiped her eyes with her fingers, rubbing off a good amount, but she could only be helped so much at this point.

Which wasn't all that much.

She grabbed her purse and got out of the car. She pulled her phone out before she slid the strap onto her shoulder and headed up the path, skimming her text messages first. She'd put her phone on silent while driving, knowing she was already distracted enough without any added help.

Paige was at the top: *I love you. You've got this. You're amazing.*

Her mother was next: *Just checking on u. Call 2nite. Please.*

Then Gemma: *Let me know if you want to get a drink to talk.*

Paige again: *A-M-A-Z-I-N-G*

And a novel from Brooke who sent the longest texts of life: *Everything completely cleared out of the office. I grabbed your blender out of the kitchen. Gemma already sent me the new hire paperwork. I printed it out and put it in your mailbox at home. Your mom called me to check up on you and I told her that you were okay. And Logan dropped by before I left looking for you…*

Abby stopped short as she reread those words three times, and then her eyes finally moved on to finish the text.

...He wanted to know where you were so I told him you'd gone to Mirabelle and that you'd be back today. Pretty sure he's going to show up at your house. Just so you know. Call if you need anything.

She felt eyes on her a second before her head came up. And there he was, standing at her front door with a bottle of Jack Daniel's in his hand.

* * *

Logan hadn't exactly been prepared for the physical pain that was seeing Abby. There were many different components to it.

One was being so close and not getting to put his hands on her, she was only feet away. This was something he'd experienced many times over the last few months, but it was different today. There was a distance between them that had nothing to do with physical space and it had to be breached first.

Two was he missed her. Missed her so fucking much. Four days. Four days without her. Four days thinking it was over. Four days of being a miserable asshole.

The kicker to it all? The pain that was the worst? Seeing how much he'd hurt her. She already had a fair complexion, but today her skin was paler than pale. Her shoulders were slumped, like she was about to cave in on herself. Her blue eyes red rimmed, her makeup a mess beyond anything he'd ever seen.

But she was his mess. His beautiful mess.

"Hi." Her voice cracked on the word and he was pretty sure his heart had as well. "How long..." she whispered thickly, the words getting stuck. She shook her head before she tried again. "How long have you been here?"

"About an hour. Brooke didn't know when you were getting back. I was prepared to sit out here all night."

"All by yourself?"

"I have Jack," he said, holding up the bottle that was in his hand. "He's great company."

"What are you planning on doing with that?" A small smile tugged the very corner of her mouth, but it didn't get any further.

"I thought we could talk."

"About?"

"Everything. Open the door, Red. Let's go inside."

She nodded and moved past him. He wanted more than anything to reach out and touch her, wanted to pull her into his chest and press his nose to her hair to inhale her. But he'd just have to make do with the subtle scent of her shampoo on the air when she walked by.

It wasn't enough.

The lock clicked and they stepped inside.

Again he had to consciously stop himself from closing the small space between them. Had to stop himself from putting his hands around her waist and leaning down to kiss her neck.

She walked through the hallway and to the living room. He went to the dining room table where he set the bottle of Jack down while Abby settled her things on the sofa. She hesitated for just a second, taking a deep breath, before she turned to look at him. Her eyes met his, a wealth of sadness in those deep blue depths.

"Brooke told me that you actually quit the Stampede before you were fired."

"Yeah." She braced her hand on the back of the sofa as she shifted from one foot to the other.

"Truth: *why* did you quit?"

She stopped fidgeting and her breath caught in her throat, her entire body freezing for just a moment. He was sure it was the phrasing of his question that caught her off guard, and he didn't miss the hope that flared in her eyes. It took her a second to find her voice.

"Many reasons. But mainly? Because I couldn't be with you and do my job at the same time. The information on Madison in your file wasn't the first place I came across it. I found the pictures of her in your dresser when I was looking for my clothes."

"You did?" That was new information. Information he didn't know how to feel about.

"She was beautiful you know? Madison. She was a stunning little girl, looked so much like you. And she was somebody that I wanted to protect, too. I picked you, Logan. I chose you. I shredded the stuff on her that was in your file. I quit because I wanted to be with you. I realized it was an all or nothing thing, so either way I had to leave. I couldn't get the *all* working there, couldn't be with you in every way doing that job. And I didn't think that the relationship was going to work if we couldn't fully be together."

"So all or nothing."

"All or nothing." She nodded. She made a move to go to him, but her step faltered. She was unsure of herself. Unsure of him. So instead of reaching for him she continued to hold on to the sofa for balance. "I'm sorry, Logan. I never, ever wanted that to happen." She shook her head, her bottom lip trembling as tears welled in her eyes. Her gaze dropped, and her hand tightened on the back of the sofa, her fingers pressing into the stuffed gray fabric.

He crossed the space to her, closing the distance between them. His palms itched to feel her and he gave into his instinct, reaching out and running his hands up her arms. He pulled her to him, her hold on the sofa moving to a hold on him, her hands fisting in the fabric of his shirt.

She looked up at him, the tears falling freely from her eyes now. He moved one of his hands to her face, running his fingers across her cheeks and wiping away the fresh tracks that trailed down her skin.

"I know that you didn't want that to happen."

"You do?"

"Yeah, I do. And I'm sorry, too, sorry for all of it. I should've given you the chance to explain. I shouldn't have walked away, an action I won't be repeating. Because you are my future, Abby."

Her sharp inhale of breath had her entire body moving with the action. "I am?"

"God I hope so. Because having hope for the future is something that I haven't really thought of in years. Something I didn't care to think about again until I met you. But I want that with you. I want it all. *Nothing*? That isn't an option."

He leaned down, the need to taste her lips overwhelming everything else. And the second his mouth was on hers, he never wanted to stop. Her hands were in his hair as she eagerly accepted his kisses. His arms wrapped around her back, pulling her off the ground easily and sitting her down on the back of the sofa.

"Truth: when I was nineteen years old, I got my girlfriend pregnant. Cassidy never wanted Madison, and made that point perfectly clear. But I loved my daughter from the day I found out about her. She was perfect. Sweet and beautiful and kind. She was everything to me."

He let go of Abby, something that was beyond painful in that moment, and took a step back. But he had to do this, had to remove all the barriers, tell her everything. He reached behind him, grabbing a fistful of his shirt before he pulled it off and threw it to the ground.

"Truth: the tattoo on my back is not for Michigan. It's for Madison." He turned slightly so Abby could see his shoulder blade.

She reached out, not saying anything as she traced the black ink on his skin. He closed his eyes, swallowing hard as he savored her touch, focused on the path of her fingers. Up then down, then up and down again.

"Whenever I'd wear anything with the M on it, she'd say *M for Madison* and giggle like crazy. So it's for her. Truth: she was my life and when she died it destroyed me."

He opened his eyes as he turned to look at Abby again. When her hand fell from his shoulder, he felt the absence of her touch everywhere. So he grabbed her hand, bringing it to his mouth and placing a kiss on her palm. He put it over his heart as he took a step forward, making space between her legs. He reached down with his free hand holding on to her waist for dear life, because if he held on to her he could do this.

"She was four when she was diagnosed. She was a little uncoordinated, couldn't walk on the sidewalk without finding a crack. But more and more bruises started to show up, so I took her to the doctor." His eyes burned and his throat constricted. "Six months, that's how long she had after she was diagnosed. Cassidy was long gone, and I had my parents and Adele and Liam, but my daughter was gone. She was just gone."

He blinked, the tears falling.

"Logan," she whispered as she reached up, her hand cradling his jaw.

"Truth," he said as he leaned into her touch. "You brought me out of a darkness that I've been living in for eight years. Made me feel something again. So many moments that had my heart beating out of my chest." He gently squeezed the hand that was still placed over his heart. "The night of the charity dinner and you walked in wearing the sexiest red dress I think I've ever seen in my life. When we were in Mirabelle and I found you on the other side of the door at the inn. The first time I saw you when you walked into the Stampede locker room. But I think the real moment was when you crawled up on my lap at the cabin and told me I could have my way with you. That was when it happened."

"When what happened?" She rasped her thumb across his stubbled beard as she looked up at him.

"When I fell in love with you. It just took me this long to figure it out."

"Truth: that's when I fell in love with you too."

At her words his heart kicked hard in his chest, proving his point exactly. She made him feel alive again. He lowered his head, his mouth hovering inches above hers.

"Truth: you're it for me, Abby Fields."

"Truth: as you are for me."

He opened his mouth over hers, sealing their words with a kiss.

Epilogue

Strip, Shoot, or Truth . . . Part Two

Valentine's Day: One Year Later

Abby Fields grinned as she stared across the table at Logan James, trying to figure out how anything that had happened in the last year was even possible.

But it had been the best year of her life.

She was madly in love with a gorgeous man, living with him in a beautiful house in Jacksonville, and currently half-naked in a cabin with said man in the mountains of Tennessee. Snow fell steadily right outside the window, a blanket of white. But she was nice and warm in her bright red lace panties and bra, complete with garter belt.

The heat had a lot to do with the fire that blazed behind them, but she attributed the flush to her skin to the man sitting on the other side of the table. Logan was just down to his jeans, one more strip and he would be gloriously naked.

He shifted in his seat, the firelight making his skin glow as he moved, and leaned back folding his arms across his chest. He gave her that wicked grin, the one that promised it was only going to be a matter of time before she was flat on her back and he was pushing inside of her. It was the same one he'd given her on the private jet they'd taken up here, the flight that initiated the pair of them into the mile-high club.

Logan had insisted that they come up to the cabin on the anniversary of their first night together. The Stampede had won an early game that morning, and as they had a day off before their next practice, he wanted the time with her in the snowy mountains.

All alone.

Who was she to argue?

It was different being in a relationship with him when she wasn't constantly traveling with the team. They made time where they could, when they could. She was able to fly out for some of the away games and spend a few nights with Logan on the road. Gemma was pretty understanding and Abby was able to get her work done from a hotel room, no problem. Plus Brooke was awesome, and just as efficient as ever.

And as it turned out, Logan and Abby still spent a lot of time together for work. Logan had started a charity in Madison's name. He was in and out of the hospital pretty often, visiting Abby for lunch and the patients in the cancer ward with Jace and Andre and quite a few of the other players. Most of the kids were too young to recognize them as Stanley Cup winners, not knowing anything about hockey.

But Logan had never cared about the fame. A fact that made her love him all the more.

"So what's it going to be, Red?"

Her eyes darted to the shot glass in front of her, where what had to be a three-karat diamond ring glistened. It had an intricate band, forming figure eights all around, and tiny diamonds in the gaps on either side.

Abby stood up and reached for the glass, fishing the diamond ring out and wrapping it tightly in her fist. She walked to the other side of the table, her red heels echoing across the wood with each step.

Logan scooted his chair back, giving her just enough space to stand in front of him. She climbed up onto his lap and straddled him, settling herself on the erection straining the front of his jeans.

"I'll never get over seeing you in red lace," he said as he skimmed his palms up her thighs.

"Good." She grinned as she grabbed one of his hands from its upward ascent. She pulled it between them, placing the ring in the center. "Ask me again."

His hand closed over the ring and he moved, wrapping his arms around her as he stood. His chair slid back along the wooden floors, and he sat her down on top of the table.

A second later his lips were covering hers, his tongue dipping inside her mouth. And then he was pulling back, his body lowering as he got down on one knee in front of her. He grabbed her left hand, sliding the ring onto her finger before he looked up into her face.

"Truth: I want to spend the rest of my life with you. I want to celebrate every victory with you and commiserate every lose. And not just the ones out on the ice, but everything. Every day. Me and you. Marry me, Red."

She wrapped her fingers around his wrists and tugged. He came up willingly, standing between her thighs. She reached for his face, gently rasping his beard with her nails.

"Yes, I'll marry you, Logan James. And yes to everything else. Yes to all of it."

All of it.

Things Paige Morrison will never understand
about Mirabelle, Florida:

Why wearing red shoes makes a girl a harlot
Why a shop would ever sell something called "buck urine"
Why everywhere she goes, she runs into sexy—and
infuriating—Brendan King

Please see the next page for an excerpt from

Undone,

Book #1 in the Country Roads series

Chapter 1

Short Fuses and a Whole Lot of Sparks

Bethelda Grimshaw was a snot-nosed wench. She was an evil, mean-spirited, vindictive, horrible human being.

Paige should've known. She should've known the instant she walked into that office and sat down. Bethelda Grimshaw had a malevolent stench radiating off her, kind of like road kill in ninety-degree weather. The interview, if it could even be called that, had been a complete waste of time.

"She didn't even read my résumé," Paige said, slamming her hand against the steering wheel as she pulled out of the parking lot of the Mirabelle Information Center.

No, Bethelda had barely even looked at said résumé before she'd set it down on the desk and leaned back in her chair, appraising Paige over her cat's-eye glasses.

"So you're the *infamous* Paige Morrison," Bethelda had said, raising a perfectly plucked, bright red eyebrow. "You've caused *quite* a stir since you came to town."

Quite a stir?

Okay, so there had been that incident down at the Piggly Wiggly, but that hadn't been Paige's fault. Betty Whitehurst might seem like a sweet, little old lady, but in reality she was as blind as a bat and as vicious as a shrew. Betty drove her shopping cart like she was racing in the Indy 500, which was an accomplishment as she barely cleared the handle. She'd slammed her cart into Paige, who in turn fell into a display of cans. Paige had been calm for all of about five seconds before Betty started screeching at her about watching where she was going.

Paige wasn't one to take things lying down covered in cans of creamed corn, so she'd calmly explained to Betty that she *had* been watching where she was going. "Calmly" being that Paige had started yelling and the store manager had to get involved to quiet everyone down.

Yeah, Paige didn't deal very well with certain types of people. Certain types being evil, mean-spirited, vindictive, horrible human beings. And Bethelda Grimshaw was quickly climbing to the top of that list.

"As it turns out," Bethelda had said, pursing her lips in a patronizing pout, "we already filled the position. I'm afraid there was a mistake in having you come down here today."

"When?"

"Excuse me?" Bethelda had asked, her eyes sparkling with glee.

"When did you fill the position?" Paige repeated, trying to stay calm.

"Last week."

Really? So the phone call Paige had gotten that morning to confirm the time of the interview had been a mistake?

This was the eleventh job interview she'd gone on in the last two months. And it had most definitely been the worst. It hadn't even been an interview. She'd been set up; she just didn't understand why. But she hadn't been about to ask that question out loud. So instead of flying off the handle and losing her last bit of restraint, Paige had calmly gotten up from the chair and left without making a scene. The whole thing was a freaking joke, which fit perfectly for the current theme of Paige's life.

Six months ago, Paige had been living in Philadelphia. She had a good job in the art department of an advertising agency. She shared a tiny two-bedroom apartment above a coffee shop with her best friend, Abby Fields. And she had Dylan, a man she had been very much in love with.

And then the rug got pulled out from under her and she'd fallen flat on her ass.

First off, Abby got a job at an up-and-coming PR firm. Which was good news, and Paige had been very excited for her, except the job was in Washington, D.C., which Paige was not excited about. Then, before Paige could find a new roommate, she'd lost her job. The advertising agency was bought out and she was in the first round of cuts. Without a job, she couldn't renew her lease, and was therefore homeless. So she'd moved in with Dylan. It was always supposed to be a temporary thing, just until Paige could find another job and get on her feet again.

But it never happened.

Paige had tried for two months and found nothing, and then the real bomb hit. She was either blind or just distracted by everything else that was going on, but either way, she never saw it coming.

Paige had been with Dylan for about a year and she really thought he was the one. Okay, he tended to be a bit of a snob when it came to certain things. For example, wine. Oh was he ever a wine snob, rather obnoxious about it really. He would always swirl it around in his glass, take a sip, sniff, and then take another loud sip, smacking his lips together.

He was also a snob about books. Paige enjoyed reading the classics, but she also liked reading romance, mystery, and fantasy. Whenever she would curl up with one of her books, Dylan tended to give her a rather patronizing look and shake his head.

"Reading fluff again I see," he would always say.

Yeah, she didn't miss *that* at all. Or the way he would roll his eyes when she and Abby would quote movies and TV shows to each other. Or how he'd never liked her music and flat-out refused to dance with her. Which had always been frustrating because Paige loved to dance. But despite all of that, she'd loved him. Loved the way he would run his fingers through his hair when he was distracted, loved his big goofy grin, and loved the way his glasses would slide down his nose.

But the thing was, he hadn't loved her.

One night, he'd come back to his apartment and sat Paige down on the couch. Looking back on it, she'd been an idiot, because there was a small part of her that thought he was actually about to propose.

"Paige," he'd said, sitting down on the coffee table and grabbing her hands. "I know that this was supposed to be a temporary thing, but weeks have turned into months. Living with you has brought a lot of things to light."

It was wrong, everything about that moment was *all wrong*. She could tell by the look in his eyes, by the tone of his voice, by the way he said *Paige* and *light*. In that moment she'd known exactly where he was going, and it wasn't anywhere with her. He wasn't proposing. He was breaking up with her.

She'd pulled her hands out of his and shrank back into the couch.

"This," he'd said, gesturing between the two of them, "was never going to go further than where we are right now."

And that was the part where her ears had started ringing.

"At one point I thought I might love you, but I've realized I'm not *in* love with you," he'd said, shaking his head. "I feel like you've thought this was going to go further, but the truth is I'm never going to marry you. Paige, you're not the one. I'm tired of pretending. I'm tired of putting in the effort for a relationship that isn't going anywhere else. It's not worth it to me."

"You mean I'm not worth it," she'd said, shocked.

"Paige, you deserve to be with someone who wants to make the effort, and I deserve to be with someone who I'm willing to make the effort for. It's better that we end this now, instead of delaying the inevitable."

He'd made it sound like he was doing her a favor, like he had her best interests at heart.

But all she'd heard was *You're not worth it* and *I'm not in love with you.* And those were the words that kept repeating in her head, over and over and over again.

Dylan had told her he was going to go stay with one of his friends for the week. She'd told him she'd be out before the end of the next day. She'd spent the entire night packing up her stuff. Well, packing and crying and drinking two entire bottles of the prick's wine.

Paige didn't have a lot of stuff. Most of the furniture from her and Abby's apartment had been Abby's. Everything that Paige owned had fit into the back of her Jeep and the U-Haul trailer that she'd rented the first thing the following morning. She'd loaded up and gotten out of there before four o'clock in the afternoon.

She'd stayed the night in a hotel room just outside of Philadelphia, where she'd promptly passed out. She'd been exhausted after her marathon packing, which was good because it was harder for a person to feel beyond pathetic in her sleep. No, that was what the following eighteen-hour drive had been reserved for.

Jobless, homeless, and brokenhearted, Paige had nowhere else to go but home to her parents. The problem was, there was no *home* anymore. The house in Philadelphia that Paige had grown up in was no longer her parents'. They'd sold it and retired to a little town in the South.

Mirabelle, Florida: population five thousand.

There was roughly the same amount of people in the six hundred square miles of Mirabelle as there were in half a square mile of Philadelphia. Well, unless the mosquitoes were counted as residents.

People who thought that Florida was all sunshine and sand were sorely mistaken. It did have its fair share of beautiful beaches. The entire southeast side of Mirabelle was the Gulf of Mexico. But about half of the town was made up of water. And all of that water, combined with the humidity that plagued the area, created the perfect breeding ground for mosquitoes. Otherwise known as tiny, blood-sucking villains that loved to bite the crap out of Paige's legs.

Paige had visited her parents a couple of times over the last couple of years, but she'd never been in love with Mirabelle like her parents were. And she still wasn't. She'd spent a month moping around her parents' house. Again, she was pathetic enough to believe that maybe, just maybe, Dylan would call her and tell her that he'd been wrong. That he missed her. That he loved her.

He never called, and Paige realized he was never going to. That was when Paige resigned herself to the fact that she had to move on with her life. So she'd started looking for a job.

Which had proved to be highly unsuccessful.

Paige had been living in Mirabelle for three months now.

Three long miserable months where nothing had gone right. Not one single thing.

And as that delightful thought crossed her mind, she noticed that her engine was smoking. Great white plumes of steam escaped from the hood of her Jeep Cherokee.

"You've got to be kidding me," she said as she pulled off to the side of the road and turned the engine off. "Fan-freaking-tastic."

Paige grabbed her purse and started digging around in the infinite abyss, searching for her cell phone. She sifted through old receipts, a paperback book, her wallet, lip gloss, a nail file, gum... *ah*, cell phone. She pressed the speed dial for her father. She held the phone against her ear while she leaned over and searched for her shoes that she'd thrown on the floor of the passenger side. As her hand closed over one of her black wedges, the phone beeped in her ear and disconnected. She sat up and held her phone out, staring at the display screen in disbelief.

No service.

"This has to be some sick, twisted joke," she said, banging her head down on the steering wheel. No service on her cell phone shouldn't have been that surprising; there were plenty of dead zones around Mirabelle. Apparently there was a lack of cell phone towers in this little piece of purgatory.

Paige resigned herself to the fact that she was going to have to walk to find civilization, or at least a bar of service on her cell phone. She went in search of her other wedge, locating it under the passenger seat.

The air conditioner had been off for less than two minutes, and it was already starting to warm up inside the Jeep. It was going to be a long, hot walk. Paige grabbed a hair tie from the gearshift, put her long brown hair up into a messy bun, and opened the door to the sweltering heat.

I hate this godforsaken place.

Paige missed Philadelphia. She missed her friends, her apartment with its rafters and squeaky floors. She missed having a job, missed having a paycheck, missed buying shoes. And even though she hated it, she still missed Dylan. Missed his dark shaggy hair and the way he would nibble on her lower lip when they kissed. She even missed his humming when he cooked.

She shook her head and snapped back to the present. She might as well focus on the task at hand and stop thinking about what was no longer her life.

Paige walked for twenty minutes down the road to nowhere, not a single car passing her. By the time Paige got to Skeeter's Bait, Tackle, Guns, and Gas, she was sweating like nobody's business, her dress was sticking to her everywhere, and her feet were killing her. She had a nice blister on the back of her left heel.

She pushed the door open and was greeted with the smell of fish mixed with bleach, making her stomach turn. At least the air conditioner was cranked to full blast. There was a huge stuffed turkey sitting on the counter. The fleshy red thing on its neck looked like the stuff nightmares were made of, and the wall behind the register was covered in mounted fish. She really didn't get the whole "dead animal as a trophy" motif that the South had going on.

There was a display on the counter that had tiny little bottles that looked like energy drinks.

NEW AND IMPROVED SCENT. GREAT FOR ATTRACTING THE PERFECT GAME.

She picked up one of the tiny bottles and looked at it. It was doe urine.

She took a closer look at the display. They apparently also had the buck urine variety. She looked at the bottle in her hand, trying to grasp why people would cover themselves in this stuff. Was hunting really worth smelling like an animal's pee?

"Can I help you?"

The voice startled Paige and she looked up into the face of a very large balding man, his apron covered in God only knew what. She dropped the tiny bottle she had in her hand. It fell to the ground. The cap smashed on the tile floor and liquid poured out everywhere.

It took a total of three seconds for the smell to punch her in the nose. It had to be the most fowl scent she'd ever inhaled.

Oh crap. Oh crap, oh crap, oh crap.

She was just stellar at first impressions these days.

"I'm so sorry," she said, trying not to gag. She took a step back from the offending puddle and looked up at the man.

His arms were folded across his chest and he frowned at her, saying nothing.

"Do you, uh, have something I can clean this up with?" she asked nervously.

"You're not from around here," he said, looking at her with his deadpan stare. It wasn't a question. It was a statement, one that she got whenever she met someone new. One that she was so sick and tired of she could scream. Yeah, all of the remorse she'd felt over spilling that bottle drained from her.

In Philadelphia, Paige's bohemian style was normal, but in Mirabelle her big earrings, multiple rings, and loud clothing tended to get her noticed. Her parents' neighbor, Mrs. Forns, thought that Paige was trouble, which she complained about on an almost daily basis.

"You know that marijuana is still illegal," Mrs. Forns had said the other night, standing on her parents' porch and lecturing Paige's mother. "And I won't hesitate to call the authorities if I see your hippie daughter growing anything suspicious or doing any other illegal activities."

Denise Morrison, ever the queen of politeness, had just smiled. "You have nothing to be concerned about."

"But she's doing *something* in that shed of yours in the backyard."

The *something* that Paige did in the shed was paint. She'd converted it into her art studio, complete with ceiling fan.

"Don't worry, Mrs. Forns," Paige had said, sticking her head over her mother's shoulder. "I'll wait to have my orgies on your bingo nights. Is that on Tuesdays or Wednesdays?"

"Paige!" Denise had said as she'd shoved Paige back into the house and closed the door in her face.

Five minutes later, Denise had come into the kitchen shaking her head.

"Really, Paige? You had to tell her that you're having *orgies* in the backyard?"

Paige's father, Trevor Morrison, chuckled as he went through the mail at his desk.

"You need to control your temper and that smart mouth of yours," Denise had said.

"You know what you should start doing?" Trevor said, looking up with a big grin. "You should grow oregano in pots on the windowsill and then throw little dime bags into her yard."

"Trevor, don't encourage her harassing that woman. Paige, she's a little bit older, very set in her ways, and a tad bit nosey."

"She needs to learn to keep her nose on her side of the fence," Paige had said.

"Don't let her bother you."

"That's easier said than done."

"Well then, maybe you should practice holding your tongue."

"Yes, Mother, I'll get right on that."

So, as Paige stared at the massive man in front of her, whom she assumed to be Skeeter, she pursed her lips and held back the smart-ass retort that was on the tip of her tongue.

Be polite, she heard her mother's voice in her head say. *You just spilled animal pee all over his store. And you need to use his phone.*

"No," Paige said, pushing her big sunglasses up her nose and into her hair. "My car broke down and I don't have any cell phone service. I was wondering if I could use your phone to call a tow truck."

"I'd call King's if I were you. They're the best," he said as he ripped a piece of receipt paper off the cash register and grabbed a pen with a broken plastic spoon taped to the top. He wrote something down and pushed the paper across the counter.

"Thank you. I can clean that up first," she said, pointing to the floor.

"I got it. I'd hate for you to get those hands of yours dirty," he said, moving the phone to her side of the counter.

She just couldn't win.

* * *

Brendan King leaned against the front bumper of Mr. Thame's minivan. He was switching out the old belt and replacing it with a new one when his grandfather stuck his head out of the office.

"Brendan," Oliver King said, "a car broke down on Buckland Road. It's Paige Morrison, Trevor and Denise Morrison's daughter. She said the engine was smoking. She had to walk to Skeeter's to use the phone. I told her you'd pick her up so she didn't have to walk back."

Oliver King didn't look his seventy years. His salt-and-pepper hair was still thick and growing only on the top of his head, and not out of his ears. He had a bit of a belly, but he'd had that for the last twenty years and it wasn't going anywhere. He'd opened King's Auto forty-three years ago, when he was twenty-seven. Now, he mainly worked behind the front counter, due to the arthritis in his hands and back. But it was a good thing because King's Auto was one of only a handful of auto shops in the county. They were always busy, so they needed a constant presence running things out of the shop.

Including Brendan and his grandfather, there were four full-time mechanics and two part-time kids who were still in high school and who worked in the garage. Part of the service that King's provided was towing, and Brendan was the man on duty on Mondays. And oh was he ever so happy he was on duty today.

Paige Morrison was the new girl in town. Her parents had moved down from Pennsylvania when they retired about two years ago, and Paige had moved in with them three months ago. Brendan had yet to meet her but he'd most definitely seen her. You couldn't really miss her as she jogged around town, with her very long legs, in a wide variety of the brightest and shortest shorts he'd ever seen in his life. His favorite pair had by far been the hot-pink pair, but the zebra-print ones came in a very close second.

He'd also heard about her. People had a lot to say about her more-than-*interesting* style. It was rumored that she had a bit of a temper and a pretty mouth that said whatever it wanted. Not that Brendan took a lot of stock in gossip. He'd wait to reserve his own judgment.

"Got it," Brendan said, pulling his gloves off and sticking them in his back pocket. "Tell Randall this still needs new spark plugs," he said, pointing to the minivan and walking into the office.

"I will." Oliver nodded and handed Brendan the keys to the tow truck.

Brendan grabbed two waters from the mini-fridge and his sunglasses from the desk and headed off into the scorching heat. It was a hot one, ninety-eight degrees, but the humidity made it feel like one hundred and three. He flipped his baseball cap so that the bill would actually give him some cover from the August sun, and when he got into the tow truck he cranked the air as high as it would go.

It took him about fifteen minutes to get to Skeeter's, and when he pulled up into the gravel parking lot, the door to the little shop opened and Brendan couldn't help smiling.

Paige Morrison's mile-long legs were shooting out of the sexiest shoes he'd ever seen. She was also wearing a flowing yellow dress that didn't really cover her amazing legs but did hug her chest and waist, and besides the two skinny straps at her shoulders, her arms were completely bare. Massive sunglasses covered her eyes and her dark brown hair was piled on top of her head.

There was no doubt about it; she was beautiful all right.

Brendan put the truck in Park and hopped out.

"Ms. Morrison?" he asked even though he already knew who she was.

"Paige," she corrected, stopping in front of him. She was probably five-foot-ten or so, but her shoes added about three inches, making her just as tall as him. If he wasn't wearing his work boots she would've been taller than him.

"I'm Brendan King," he said, sticking his hand out to shake hers. Her hand was soft and warm. He liked how it felt in his. He also liked the freckles that were sprinkled across her high cheekbones and straight, pert nose.

"I'm about a mile up the road," she said, letting go of his hand and pointing in the opposite direction that he'd come.

"Not the most sensible walking shoes," he said, eyeing her feet.

The toes that peeked out of her shoes were bright red, and a thin band of silver wrapped around the second toe on her right foot. He looked back up to see her arched eyebrows come together for a second before she took a deep breath.

"Thanks for the observation," she said, walking past him and heading for the passenger door.

Well, this was going to be fun.

* * *

Stupid jerk.

Not the most sensible walking shoes, Paige repeated in her head. *Well, no shit, Sherlock.*

Paige sat in the cab of Brendan's tow truck, trying to keep her temper in check. Her feet were killing her, and she really wanted to kick off her shoes. But she couldn't do that in front of him because then he would *know* that her feet were killing her.

"I'm guessing the orange Jeep is yours?" Brendan asked as it came into view.

"Another outstanding observation," she mumbled under her breath.

"I'm sorry?"

"Yes, it's mine," she said, trying to hide her sarcasm.

"Well, at least the engine isn't smoking anymore," he said as he pulled in behind it and jumped out of the truck. Paige grabbed her keys from her purse and followed, closing the door behind her.

He stopped behind the back of her Jeep for a moment, studying the half a dozen stickers that covered her bumper and part of her back window.

She had one that said MAKE ART NOT WAR in big blue letters,

another said LOVE with a peace sign in the *O*. There was also a sea turtle, an owl with reading glasses, the Cat in the Hat, and her favorite that said I LOVE BIG BOOKS AND I CANNOT LIE.

He shook his head and laughed, walking to the front of the Jeep.

"What's so funny?" she asked, catching up to his long stride and standing next to him.

"Keys?" he asked, holding out his hand.

She put them in his palm but didn't let go.

"What's so funny?" she repeated.

"Just that you're clearly not from around here." He smiled, closing his hand over hers.

Brendan had a southern accent, not nearly as thick as some of the other people's in town, and a wide cocky smile that she really hated, but only because she kind of liked it. She also kind of liked the five-o'clock shadow that covered his square jaw. She couldn't see anything above his chiseled nose, as half of his face was covered by his sunglasses and the shadow from his grease-stained baseball cap, but she could tell his smile reached all the way up to his eyes.

He was most definitely physically fit, filling out his shirt and pants with wide biceps and thighs. His navy blue button-up shirt had short sleeves, showing off his tanned arms that were covered in tiny blond hairs.

God, he was attractive. But he was also pissing her off.

"I am so sick of everyone saying that," she said, ripping her hand out of his. "Is it such a bad thing to not be from around here?"

"No," he said, his mouth quirking. "It's just very obvious that you're not."

"Would I fit in more if I had a bumper sticker that said MY OTHER CAR IS A TRACTOR or one that said IF YOU'RE NOT CONSERVATIVE YOU JUST AREN'T WORTH IT, or what about

Who needs literacy when you can shoot things? What if I had a gun rack mounted on the back window or if I used buck piss as perfume to attract a husband? Would those things make me fit in?" she finished, folding her arms across her chest.

"No, I'd say you could start with not being so judgmental though," he said with a sarcastic smirk.

"Excuse me?"

"Ma'am, you just called everyone around here gun-toting, illiterate rednecks who like to participate in bestiality. Insulting people really isn't a way to fit in," he said, shaking his head. "I would also refrain from spreading your liberal views to the masses, as politics are a bit of a hot-button topic around here. And if you want to attract a husband, you should stick with wearing doe urine, because that attracts only males. The buck urine attracts both males and females." He stopped and looked her up and down with a slow smile. "But maybe you're into that sort of thing."

"Yeah, well, everyone in this town thinks that I'm an amoral, promiscuous pothead. And you," she said, shoving her finger into his chest, "aren't any better. People make snap judgments about me before I even open my mouth. And just so you know, *I'm not even a liberal,*" she screamed as she jabbed her finger into his chest a couple of times. She took a deep breath and stepped back, composing herself. "So maybe I would be *nice* if people would be just a little bit *nice* to me."

"I'm quite capable of being nice to people who deserve it. Can I look at your car now, or would you like to yell at me some more?"

"Be my guest," she said, glaring at him as she moved out of his way.

He unlocked the Jeep and popped the hood. As he moved to the front he pulled off his baseball cap and wiped the top of his head with his hand. Paige glimpsed his short, dirty-blond hair before he put the hat on backward. As he moved around in her engine his shirt pulled tight across his back and shoulders. He twisted off the cap to something and stuck it in his pocket. Then he walked back to his truck and grabbed a jug from a metal box on the side. He came back and poured the liquid into something in the engine and after a few seconds it gushed out of the bottom.

"Your radiator is cracked," he said, grabbing the cap out of his pocket and screwing it back on. "I'm going to have to tow this back to the shop to replace it."

"How much?"

"For everything? We're looking at four maybe five hundred."

"Just perfect," she mumbled.

"Would you like a ride? Or were you planning on showing those shoes more of the countryside?"

"I'll take the ride."

* * *

Paige was quiet the whole time Brendan loaded her Jeep onto the truck. Her arms were folded under her perfect breasts and she stared at him with her full lips bunched in a scowl. Even pissed off she was stunning, and God, that mouth of hers. He really wanted to see it with an actual smile on it. He was pretty sure it would knock him on his ass.

Speaking of asses, seeing her smile probably wasn't likely at the moment. True, he had purposefully egged her on, but he couldn't resist going off on her when she'd let loose her colorful interpretations of the people from the area. A lot of them were true, but there was a difference between making fun of your own people and having an outsider make fun of them. But still, according to her, the people around here hadn't exactly been nice to her.

Twenty minutes later, with Paige's Jeep on the back of the tow truck, they were on their way to the shop. Brendan glanced over at her as he drove. She was looking out the window with her back to him. Her shoulders were stiff and she looked like she'd probably had enough stress before her car had decided to die on her.

Brendan looked back at the road and cleared his throat.

"I'm sorry about what I said back there."

Out of the corner of his eye he saw her shift in her seat, and he could feel her eyes on him.

"Thank you. I should have kept my mouth shut, too. I just haven't had the best day."

"Why?" he asked, glancing over at her again.

Her body was angled toward him, but her arms were still folded across her chest like a shield. He couldn't help glancing down and seeing that her dress was slowly riding up her thighs. She had nice thighs, soft but strong. They would be good for... well, a lot of things.

He quickly looked back at the road, thankful he was wearing sunglasses.

"I've been trying to get a job. Today I had an interview, except it wasn't much of an interview."

"What was it?" he asked.

"A setup."

"A setup for what?"

"That *is* the question," she said bitterly.

"Huh?" he asked, looking at her again.

"I'm assuming you know who Bethelda Grimshaw is?"

Brendan's blood pressure had a tendency to rise at the mere mention of that name. Knowing that Bethelda had a part in Paige's current mood had Brendan's temper flaring instantly.

"What did she do?" he asked darkly.

Paige's eyebrows raised a fraction at his tone. She stared at him for a second before she answered. "There was a job opening at the Mirabelle Information Center to take pictures for the brochures and the local businesses for their website. They filled the position last week, something that Mrs. Grimshaw failed to mention when she called this morning to confirm my interview."

"She's looking for her next story."

"What?"

"Bethelda Grimshaw is Mirabelle's resident gossip," Brendan said harshly as he looked back to the road. "She got fired from the newspaper a couple of years ago because of the trash she wrote. Now she has a blog to spread her crap around."

"And she wants to write about me? Why?"

"I can think of a few reasons."

"What's that supposed to mean?" she asked, her voice going up an octave or two.

"Your ability to fly off the handle. Did you give her something to write about?" he asked, raising an eyebrow as he spared a glance at her.

"No," she said, bunching her full lips together. "I saved my freak-out for you."

"I deserved it. I wasn't exactly nice to you," Brendan said, shifting his hands down the steering wheel.

"You were a jerk."

Brendan came to a stop at a stop sign and turned completely in his seat to face Paige. Her eyebrows rose high over her sunglasses and she held her breath.

"I was, and I'm sorry," he said, putting every ounce of sincerity into his words.

"It's... I forgive you," she said softly, and nodded her head.

Brendan turned back to the intersection and made a right.

Paige was silent for a few moments, but he could feel her gaze on him as if she wanted to say something.

"What?"

"Why does buck urine attract males and females?"

Brendan couldn't help smiling.

"Bucks like to fight each other," he said, looking at her.

"Oh." She nodded and leaned back in her seat staring out the front window.

"You thirsty?" Brendan asked as he grabbed one of the waters in the cup holder and held it out to her.

"Yes, thank you," she said, grabbing it and downing half the bottle.

"Who were the other interviews with?" Brendan asked, grabbing the other bottle for himself. He twisted the cap off and threw it into the cup holder.

"Landingham Printing and Design. Mrs. Landingham said I wouldn't be a good fit. Which is completely false because the program they use is one that I've used before."

Now he couldn't help laughing.

"Uh, Paige, I can tell you right now why you didn't get that job. Mrs. Landingham didn't want you around Mr. Landingham."

"What?" she said, sitting up in her seat again. "What did she think I was going to do, steal her husband? I don't make plays on married men. Or men in their forties for that matter."

"Did you wear something like what you're wearing now to the interview?" he asked, looking at her and taking another eyeful of those long legs.

"I wore a black blazer with this. It's just so hot outside that I took it off."

"Maybe you should try wearing pants next time, and flats," he said before he took a sip of water.

"What's wrong with this dress?" she asked, looking down at herself. "It isn't that short."

"Sweetheart, with those legs, anything looks short."

"Don't call me sweetheart. And it isn't my fault I'm tall."

"No, it isn't, but people think the way they think."

"So southern hospitality only goes so far when people think you're a whore."

"Hey, I didn't say that. I was just saying that your legs are long without those shoes that you're currently wearing. With them, you're pretty damn intimidating."

"Let's stop talking about my legs."

"Fine." He shrugged, looking back to the road. "But it is a rather visually stimulating conversation."

"Oh no. You are *not* allowed to flirt with me."

"Why not?"

"You were mean to me. I do *not* flirt with mean men."

"I can be nice," he said, turning to her and giving her a big smile.

"Stop it," she said, raising her eyebrows above her glasses in warning. "I mean it."

"So what about some of the other interviews? Who were they with?"

"Lindy's Frame Shop, that art gallery over on the beach—"

"Avenue Ocean?"

"Yeah, that one. And I also went to Picture Perfect. They all said I wasn't a good fit for one reason or another," she said, dejected.

"Look, I'm really not one to get involved in town gossip. I've been on the receiving end my fair share of times and it isn't fun. But this is a small town, and everybody knows one another's business. Since you're new, you have no idea. Cynthia Bowers at Picture Perfect would've never hired you. Her husband has monogamy issues. The owner of Avenue Ocean, Mindy Trist, doesn't like anyone that's competition."

"Competition?"

Mindy Trist was a man-eater. Brendan knew this to be a fact because Mindy had been trying to get into his bed for years. He wasn't even remotely interested.

"You're prettier than she is."

Understatement of the year.

Paige was suddenly silent on her side of the truck.

"And as for Hurst and Marlene Lindy," Brendan continued, "they, uh, tend to be a little more conservative."

"Look," she said, snapping out of her silence.

Brendan couldn't help himself, her sudden burst of vehemence made him look at her again. If he kept this up he was going to drive into a ditch.

"I know I might appear to be some free-spirited hippie, but I'm really not. I'm moderate when it comes to politics," she said, holding up one finger. "I eat meat like it's nobody's business." Two fingers. "And I've never done drugs in my life." Three fingers.

"You don't have to convince me," he said, shaking his head. "So I'm sensing a pattern here with all of these jobs. Are you a photographer?"

"Yes, but I do graphic design and I paint."

"So a woman of many talents."

"I don't know about that," she said, shaking her head.

"Oh, I'm sure you have a lot of talent. It's probably proportional to the length of your legs."

"What did I tell you about flirting?" she asked seriously, but betrayed herself when the corner of her mouth quirked up.

"Look, Paige, don't let it get to you. Not everyone is all bad."

"So I've just been fortunate enough to meet everyone who's mean."

"You've met me."

"Yeah, well, the jury's still out on you."

"Then I guess I'll have to prove myself."

"I guess so," she said, leaning back in her seat. Her arms now rested in her lap, her shield coming down a little.

"I have a question," Brendan said, slowing down at another stop sign. "If you eat meat, why do you have such a problem with hunting?"

"It just seems a little barbaric. Hiding out in the woods to shoot Bambi and then mounting his head on a wall."

"Let me give you two scenarios."

"Okay."

"In scenario one, we have Bessie the cow. Bessie was born in a stall, taken away from her mother shortly after birth where she was moved to a pasture for a couple of years, all the while being injected with hormones and then shoved into a semi truck where she was shipped off to be slaughtered. And I don't think that you even want me to get started on that process.

"In scenario two, we have Bambi. Bambi was born in the wilderness and wasn't taken away from his mother. He then found a mate, had babies, and one day was killed. He never saw it coming. Not only is Bambi's meat hormone free, but he also lived a happy life in the wild, with no fences.

"Now you tell me, which scenario sounds better: being raised to be slaughtered, or living free where you might or might not be killed?"

She was silent for a few moments before she sighed.

"Fine, you win. The second sounds better."

"Yeah, that's what I thought," Brendan said as he pulled into the parking lot of King's Auto. "How are you getting home?" he asked as he put the truck into Park.

"I called my dad after I called you. He's here actually," she said, pointing to a black Chevy Impala.

They both got out of the truck and headed toward the auto shop. Brendan held the door open for Paige, shoving his sunglasses into his shirt pocket. His grandfather and a man who Brendan recognized as Paige's father stood up from their chairs as Brendan and Paige walked in.

Trevor Morrison was a tall man, maybe six-foot-four or six-foot-five. He had light reddish-brown wispy hair on his head and large glasses perched on his nose. And like his daughter, his face and arms were covered in freckles.

"Hi, Daddy," Paige said, pushing her glasses up her nose and into her hair.

Brendan immediately noticed the change in her voice. Her cautious demeanor vanished and her shoulders relaxed. He'd caught a glimpse of this in the truck, but not to this extent.

"Mr. Morrison," Brendan said, taking a step forward and sticking his hand out.

Trevor grabbed Brendan's hand firmly. "Brendan," he said, giving him a warm smile and nodding his head. Trevor let go of Brendan's hand and turned to his daughter. "Paige, this is Oliver King," he said, gesturing to Brendan's grandfather, who was standing behind his desk. "Oliver, this is my daughter, Paige."

"I haven't had the pleasure," Oliver said, moving out from behind his desk and sticking out his hand.

Paige moved forward past Brendan, her arm brushing his as she passed.

"It's nice to meet you, sir," she said, grabbing Oliver's hand.

Oliver nodded as he let go of Paige's hand and looked up at Brendan. "So what happened?"

Paige turned to look at Brendan, too. It was the first time he'd gotten a full look at her face without her sunglasses on. She had long dark eyelashes that framed her large gray irises. It took him a second to remember how to speak. He cleared his throat and looked past her to the other two men.

"It's the radiator. I'm going to have to order a new one, so it's going to take a few days."

"That's fine," she said, shrugging her shoulders. "It's not like I have anywhere to go."

Trevor's face fell. "The interview didn't go well?"

"Nope," Paige said, shaking her head. The tension in her shoulders came back but she tried to mask it by pasting a smile on her face. He desperately wanted to see a genuine, full-on smile from her.

"Things haven't exactly gone Paige's way since she moved here," Trevor said.

"Oh, I think my bad luck started long before I moved here," she said, folding her arms across her chest. Every time she did that it pushed her breasts up, and it took everything in Brendan not to stare.

"I don't think it was Paige's fault," Brendan said, and everyone turned to look at him. "It was with Bethelda Grimshaw," he said to Oliver.

"Oh," Oliver said, shaking his head ruefully. "Don't let anything she says get to you. She's a horrible hag."

Paige laughed and the sound of it did funny things to Brendan's stomach.

"Told you," Brendan said, looking at her. Paige turned to him, a small smile lingering on her lips and in her eyes.

God, she was beautiful.

"Things will turn around," Oliver said. "We'll call you with an estimate before we do anything to your car."

They said their goodbyes and as Paige walked out with her father, she gave Brendan one last look, her lips quirking up slightly before she shook her head and walked out the door.

"I don't believe any of that nonsense people are saying about her," Oliver said as they both watched Paige and her dad walk out. "She's lovely."

Lovely? Yeah, that wasn't exactly the word Brendan would have used to describe her.

Hot? Yes. *Fiery?* Absolutely.

"Yeah, she's something all right."

"Oh, don't tell me you aren't a fan of hers. Son, you barely took your eyes off her."

"I'm not denying she's beautiful." How could he? "I bet she's a handful though and she's got a temper on her, along with a smart mouth." But he sure did like that smart mouth.

"That's a bit of the pot calling the kettle black," Oliver said, raising one bushy eyebrow. "If all of her experiences in this town have been similar to what Bethelda dishes out, I'm not surprised she's turned on the defense. You know what it's like to be the center of less than unsavory gossip in this town. To have a lot of the people turn their backs on you and turn you into a pariah," Oliver said, giving Brendan a knowing look.

"I know," Brendan conceded. "She deserves a break."

"You should help her find a job."

"With who?"

"You'll think of something," Oliver said, patting Brendan on the shoulder before going back to his desk. "You always do."

Jax has been protecting his best friend's kid sister, Grace, since they were young. Now that they're all grown up, they insist there's nothing between them—until one night changes everything…

Please see the next page for a preview of

Undeniable.

Book #2 in the Country Roads series

Prologue

The Princess

At six years old there were certain things Grace King didn't understand. She didn't understand where babies came from, how birds flew way up high in the sky, or where her father was. Grace had never met her dad; she didn't know what he looked like, she didn't even know his name, and for some reason this fact fascinated many people in Mirabelle.

"What's a girl bastard?"

Grace looked up from the picture she was coloring to see Hoyt Reynolds and Judson Coker looming over the other side of the picnic table where she was sitting.

Every day after the bell rang, Grace would wait outside on the playground for her brother Brendan to come and get her, and they'd walk home together. Today, Brendan was running a little late.

"I don't know." Judson smirked. "I think bastard works for boys and girls."

"Yeah." Hoyt shrugged. "Trash is trash."

Brendan was always telling Grace to ignore bullies, advice he had a problem following himself. Half the time she didn't even know what they were saying. Today was no different. She had no idea what a bastard was, but she was pretty sure it wasn't anything nice.

Grace looked back down to her picture and started coloring the crown of the princess. She grabbed her pink crayon from the pile she'd dumped out on the table, and just before she started coloring the dress the picture disappeared out from under her hands.

"Hey," she protested, looking back up at the boys, "give that back."

"No, I don't think I will," Judson said before he slowly started to rip the picture.

"Stop it," Grace said, swinging her legs over the bench and getting quickly to her feet. She ran to the other side of the table and stood in front of Judson. "Give it back to me."

"Make me," he said, holding the picture up high over her head as he ripped it cleanly in half.

Grace took a step forward and stomped down hard on his foot.

"You little bitch!" Judson screamed, hopping up and down on his uninjured foot.

Grace had one second of satisfaction before she found herself sprawled out on her back, the wind knocked out of her.

"Don't ever touch her again!"

Grace looked up just in time to see a tall, freckled, red-haired boy punch Hoyt in the face. It was Jax, one of Brendan's best friends, who had come to her rescue. And boy did Jax know what he was doing, because Hoyt fell back onto his butt hard.

"And if you ever call her that word again, you'll get a lot more than a punch in the face, you stupid little scum bag," Jax said as he put himself in between Grace and Judson. "Now get out of here."

"I'm going to tell my father about this," Hoyt said. This was a legitimate threat as Hoyt's father was the principal.

"You do that." Jax shrugged.

Apparently the two eight-year-olds didn't have anything else to say and they didn't want to take their chances against a big bad eleven-year-old, because they scrambled away and ran around the side of the building and out of sight.

"You okay?" Jax asked, turning around to Grace.

It was then that Grace realized the back of her dress was covered in mud and her palms were scraped and bleeding.

"No," she sniffed before she started to bawl.

"Oh, Grace," Jax said, grabbing her under her arms and pulling her to her feet. "Come here." He pulled her into his chest and rubbed her back. "It's okay, Gracie."

She looked up at him and bit her trembling lip. "They called me names." She hiccupped.

"They weren't true," he said, looking down at her.

"What's a bastard, Jax?"

Jax's hand stilled and his nose flared. "Nothing you need to worry about," he said. "Grace, sometimes dads aren't all they're cracked up to be."

She nodded once before she buried her head back in his chest. By the time she'd cried herself out, Jax's shirt was covered in her tears. She took a step back from him and wiped her fingers underneath her eyes. Jax reached down and grabbed the two halves of her picture from the ground.

"We can tape this back together," he said, looking down at the paper. He studied it for a second before he looked back to her. "This is what you are, Grace. A princess. Don't let anyone tell you different. You understand?" he asked, lightly tugging on her blonde ponytail.

"Yes." She nodded.

"All right," he said, handing the papers back to her. "Get your stuff together and we'll go wait for Brendan."

"Where is he?" Grace asked as she gathered her crayons and put them back into the box.

"He got into trouble with Principal Reynolds again."

Grace looked up at Jax and frowned. She really didn't like the Reynolds family. Principal Reynolds wasn't any better than his son.

"No frowning, Princess. Let's go," Jax said, holding out his hand for her.

Grace shoved her crayons and drawing into her bag. She grabbed Jax's outstretched hand and let him lead her away.

About the Author

Shannon Richard grew up in the Florida Panhandle as the baby sister of two overly protective but loving brothers. She was raised by a more than somewhat eccentric mother, a self-proclaimed vocabularist who showed her how to get lost in a book, and a father who passed on his love for coffee and really loud music. She graduated from Florida State University with a BA in English literature and still lives in Tallahassee where she battles everyday life with writing, reading, and a rant every once in a while. Okay, so the rants might happen on a regular basis. She's still waiting for her Southern, scruffy, Mr. Darcy, and in the meantime writes love stories to indulge her overactive imagination. Oh, and she's a pretty big fan of the whimsy.

Learn more at:

ShannonRichard.net

Twitter, @Shan_Richard

Facebook.com/ShannonNRichard

You Might Also Like...

FOREVER

Don't miss more of Shannon Richard's critically acclaimed Country Roads series!

SHANNON RICHARD

Things Paige Morrison will never understand about Mirabelle, Florida:

Why wearing red shoes makes a girl a harlot

Why a shop would ever sell something called "buck urine"

Why everywhere she goes, she runs into sexy—and infuriating— Brendan King

After losing her job, her apartment, and her boyfriend, Paige has no choice but to leave Philadelphia and move in with her retired parents. For an artsy outsider like Paige, finding her place in the tightly knit town isn't easy—until she meets Brendan, the hot mechanic who's interested in much more than Paige's car. In no time at all, Brendan helps Paige find a new job, new friends, and a happiness she wasn't sure she'd ever feel again. With Brendan by her side, Paige finally feels like she can call Mirabelle home. But when a new bombshell drops, will the couple survive, or will their love come undone?

Their love was *undeniable*

Grace King knows two things for certain: she loves working at her grandmother's café and she loves the hunky town sheriff. She always has. As she bakes him sweet treats, Grace fantasizes about helping him work up an appetite all night long. But whenever she thinks she's finally getting somewhere, he whips out some excuse to escape. Growing up, he never looked twice at her. Now Grace won't rest until she has Jax's undivided attention.

Jaxson Anderson can't deny that his best friend's kid sister is the sexiest woman in Mirabelle, Florida. Unwilling to burden

Grace with his painful past, Jax keeps the sassy blonde at arm's length. Yet one heated kiss crumbles all of his carefully built defenses. But when a town secret surfaces, threatening to destroy everything they believe in, can the man who defended Grace from bullies as a child protect her now?

Some things you don't dare let go...

Melanie O'Bryan knows life is too short to be afraid of taking chances. And former Air Force sergeant Bennett Hart is certainly worth taking a chance on. He's agreed to help her students with a school project, but she's hoping the handsome handyman will offer her a whole lot more. Yet despite his heated glances and teasing touches, Mel senses there's something holding him back...

Bennett Hart is grateful to be alive and back home in Mirabelle, Florida. Peaceful and uncomplicated—that's all he's looking for. Until a spunky, sexy-as-hell teacher turns his life upside down. After one smoldering kiss, Bennett feels like he's falling without a parachute. But with memories of his past threatening to resurface, he'll have to decide whether to keep playing it safe, or take the biggest risk of all.

SHANNON RICHARD

One long, hot summer would never be enough…

Attorney Hannah Sterling lives a life she's worked hard for. So when she unexpectedly inherits an inn, Hannah decides to take that long overdue holiday and settle her eccentric grandmother's estate. She knew there would be challenges, but what's hardest about returning to Mirabelle, Florida, is facing the man who gave her the most passionate summer of her life—and then broke her heart.

Nathanial Shepherd never forgot the redheaded goddess who lit up his world and got away. Now that she's home, Shep vows to make up for their years apart—and if the fire in her kiss is any indication, they're well on their way. But when a devastating secret from their past threatens their future, Shep must fight to heal Hannah's heart. Because this time, their love will truly be unforgettable…

She knows the rules of the game . . .
but she can't resist his moves

Publicist Abby Fields's career is on the rise. And with failed romances in her past, she has no time for men. When a job opportunity opens up with a sports team in Florida, Abby eagerly packs up and heads south. Yet after a work event in Mirabelle, Florida, Abby finds herself in the arms of a hockey player whose heartstopping smile leads her to the steamiest night of her life . . .

Logan James is hot on and off the ice. With his team on an epic winning streak, life couldn't get better . . . until he meets Abby, the fiery redhead assigned to protect his team's image. Now Logan's finding it difficult to concentrate on anything other than getting Abby undressed. But after a secret is leaked to the press, the taste of betrayal opens old wounds. If they can't learn to trust each other, they may risk losing more than their hearts.

ISBN 978-1-4555-9044-5

90000

9 781455 590445